MOONLIGHT MATE

THE WHITE WOLF SAGA - BOOK ONE

VALIA LIND

SKAZKA PRESS

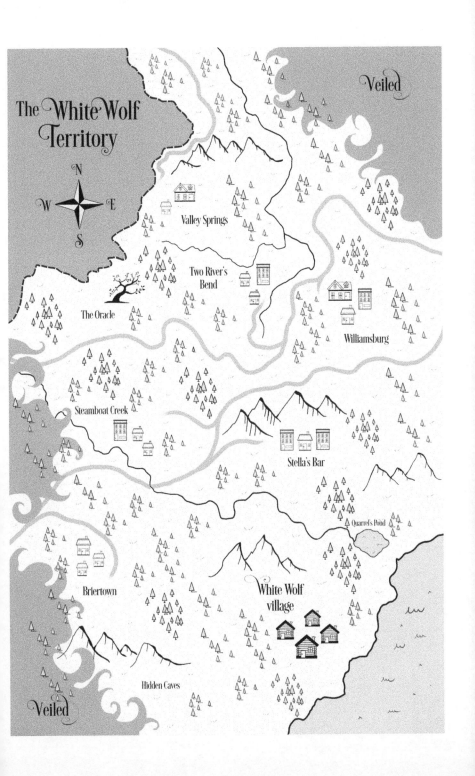

MOONLIGHT MATE

THE WHITE WOLF SAGA
BOOK ONE

CHAPTER 1

My body moves in a fluid motion, anticipating an attack a split second before it happens. A knife appears in my attacker's hand, glittering in the light of the setting sun. My attacker comes forward, slicing his arm down toward me. My shifter senses are always present, but in this case, I use my training instead of supernatural anticipation.

I duck, right under his arm, stepping out on the outside of the swing, before I kick my leg out, straight into his side. The maroon dress I'm wearing fans our around my thighs, and he reaches to grab for it, hoping to pull me back in, but I'm faster. The spot under his armpit is open because of his swing, and he stumbles to the side as I jump. There's no hesitation in my movements as I push forward, kicking at the back of his leg, driving him to his knees. When he lands, I swing my elbow down, right into his neck. At the last moment, I pull away, stepping back with a grin.

"Got you." I say, as Jay looks up at me from his position on the ground.

"You are ruthless, Trin." He grins, flicking his blade back into its handle, before getting to his feet. This man, a brother in every way but blood, is tall and tough. Which makes it so much more satisfying when I beat him. I straighten my dress and toss my long brown hair over one shoulder. I hardly ever wear it up, even during training. It's important for me to be able to handle myself when I'm not dressed in armor. Although, I always think of my dresses as a little bit of an armor. No other wolf I know loves clothes as much as I do. When I was younger, especially with my old pack, I felt ashamed of it. But not anymore.

Since coming to live with Jefferson's pack, Jay has taken a position of big brother. With his parents dead and mine gone, we both needed someone in our corner. He's been the best family I could've ever asked for. One of his responsibilities as such—his words of course—is to make sure I can take care of myself in my human form, as well as my wolf one. It's easier as a wolf, of course. Considering my senses are almost automatically synced to my surroundings. While my senses are heightened, even as a human, I try to shut them down completely when Jay and I spar. It has made me even more lethal than I already am. A badge of honor I wear proudly. Just like the dresses.

"Hey, it's not my fault you can't keep up."

"Watch it, pup. Don't forget I'm the one who taught you everything you know."

I laugh outright because we both know he did not hold back in the fight we just finished. And I still beat him. The last six years have taught me all I need to know, mostly because Jay never babied me. For which I am endlessly grateful.

When my own pack exiled me, I thought my life was over. But Jefferson, the alpha of the pack that lives on the outskirts of Hawthorne, took me in because of his friendship with my parents. That was back when they were not missing and presumed dead. I became one of his own without any hesitation. At the same time, Jay claimed me as his little sister. He worked hard to make sure I have had every opportunity given to me.

But then the Ancients happened.

Two years ago, everything in Hawthorne changed when the Ancients—the first magical beings who walked the earth and had been sleeping for generations—began waking up. The rules we lived by, the old ways of magic, blew up in our faces. Instead of keeping to ourselves, we now work directly with witches. We've studied their ways, and we discovered all kinds of history and secrets, pertaining directly to wolf shifters. Jefferson taking me in has been the best thing that's ever happened to me, and at the right time.

But that doesn't take away the sting of betrayal. My own pack should've stood by me when my parents disappeared. They never should have left me on my own. But being here with Jefferson's pack has helped heal some of those wounds.

Then again, being the only she-wolf in the two-hundred-mile radius also carries a few challenges with it. Since Jefferson's mate passed away, and I am the only female wolf around, I worried about unwanted attention. Female wolves are more rare these days. In the olden times, mates were created and traded for the pack's benefit. Thankfully, that has changed, but it still puts the pressure on me. Luckily, all of the wolf shifters in Jefferson's pack have always left me alone. Except for Jay, of course—my self appointed brother.

In the years since coming here, I have had to prove myself though. I've fought every day to convince the other wolves I was not simply a stray picked up by Jefferson out of the goodness of his heart. I'm a vital part of the pack. It's why I've trained so hard and why I've been helping out in town. I'm hoping Jefferson makes me a permanent liaison to the witches. I've not only made friends with them, but I've learned so much. After the last year especially, I feel not only part of the pack, but part of a community. That's something I wouldn't have ever dreamed about six years ago.

"So are we going again, or are you too afraid I'll beat you?" I call, flipping my hair over my shoulder and grinning at Jay.

"Always so cocky. That mouth of yours is going to get you into trouble one day."

"Sure, sure. Just say it like it is, you're afraid to lose again." I smile sweetly.

He grins, and then he moves. Anticipating his movements, I drop to my knees, sliding across the ground before I jump up behind him. He turns, and my arms come up to block his advance, when suddenly, time seems to stop.

An otherworldly sensation dumps over me like a bucket of cold water. I drop to all fours gasping just to force some air into my lungs. My chest feels heavy and full, my gaze disoriented. I can hear Jay calling out to me, but the sound is too far away. My vision swims. Right when I think I can't bear it any longer, a voice speaks loudly in my head.

"Come home."

I'm panting now, my wolf just as panicked as I am. My urge to shift is right below the surface, but I keep control, lest I lose myself to a frenzy. A face blurs in front of my vision, but just as fast as it comes, it's gone. Suddenly, I can breathe again. I raise my head to see Jay crouched in front of me, face full of concern.

"Trin?"

"I—"

But I don't finish. We feel a new sensation as one, and turn toward the forest just as our alpha, Jefferson, steps through the bushes. His eyes meet mine. There's an emotion there I don't want to acknowledge. When he speaks, my whole world shatters into a thousand pieces.

"You know."

I do. My body reacts before I think about it. I shift into my wolf form and then I run.

I RUN without any sense of direction. Just the need to get away, to outrun the call echoing inside my body. The last thing I would ever want to do is return to the place that abandoned me, to the pack who didn't stand by my side when I needed them most.

I can't return to the alpha who was my best friend. Until he wasn't.

I'm not sure how long I would've run if a noise didn't

catch my attention. Slowing down, I let my senses expand, noting the chirp of the birds and the rustle of the leaves. And then, there it is. There's heavy breathing and a few less-than-careful footsteps.

Turning in the direction of the noise, I move closer, keeping to the shadows of the trees. When I finally find the source, I nearly stumble back.

A dark brown wolf stands between two trees, about twenty feet in front of me. I've never seen him before, and when I reach out through the pack link, I can't speak to him. Not that I thought I could. After six years, I know everyone in Jefferson's pack, even those who no longer live with us.

The wolf looks around, as if he's searching for something. When he turns, I see his eyes for the first time, and my heart squeezes at the sight.

He's alone.

Not just right now, but always. I know the stories, the warnings. A lone wolf is dangerous and unpredictable. They are continuously sad and lost. It's what I would've become if Jefferson hadn't taken me in after my exile.

The worst thing a wolf can become is a lone wolf. Sometimes they lose their humanity. That last part hasn't happened in a long time, but wolves weren't meant to be alone. The feeling of having no home, no link to a pack, it's a hollow hole inside of a lone wolf's chest that can never be filled. By anything.

I take a step forward, wondering if I can find a way to help him, but then a blur of movement catches my attention. It's there and gone so fast I think I've imagined it, except the lone wolf saw it too. And he's growling at it.

The thing with no concrete shape attacks as the wolf yelps. Now I don't hesitate to spring into action. Jumping out from the cover of trees, I land just a few feet away from the fight. The creature on top of the wolf almost fazes in and out of sight. I can't tell what it is, except that it's big. It knows I'm here though. I can feel the danger surround me.

This wasn't a good idea. I'm unprepared, but I can't run now. The wolf is on the ground, bleeding from what looks like large scratches. Then, the nearly-invisible creature is on me. I yelp as a claw scratches at me. It would've gone in, but I dodged it right at the last moment. Standing on my back legs, I try to swing my front paws toward the creature, but I can't tell if I'm anywhere near it until it slams into my side, throwing me against a tree.

Wind is knocked out of my lungs. I slump for a second before I push myself up, but it's already too late. I glance at the lone wolf, hoping for some kind of help, but he's trying to crawl away.

Then, the creature is there. I see a vision of a giant talon-like claw coming toward me. I try to get out of the way, yet I know I'm moving too slow. But before the pain comes, the creature is gone. I blink and realize I'm no longer alone.

Jefferson is here. He rushed out from the trees, throwing himself between the creature and me. The smell of blood fills the air, and as I watch, I see the creature dig a claw deep into Jefferson's right shoulder.

The loudest of howls rips out of my chest and then I'm throwing my own body at the creature. Jefferson is bleeding, but he's not down. He stands tall as I land next to him, both of us growling at the creature.

From the glimpses I catch of it between its moving in and out of the trees, it looks like a bear but with bigger paws. It also has horns on top of its head that look like they don't belong there.

The creature goes to lunge at us but then stops. That's when I hear it. The rest of the pack is moving through the forest, looking for us. My howl reached them, just like I knew it would. Without hesitation, the creature leaps over us, toward the fallen lone wolf. I move toward it, but Jefferson stops me.

"He's gone, Trinity."

I look at the wolf, at the blood that now stains the ground around him, and my heart hurts. The creature picks up the wolf and disappears into the woods without a backward glance. Jefferson tumbles forward and then drops to the ground.

"Jefferson!"

Instantly, I'm at his side. The bleeding is already slowing down, but I can tell by the gash that it'll take some time to fully heal.

"Why did you do that?" I nudge his forehead with mine.

"That's what an alpha does. He protects his own," Jefferson replies. I can feel the warmth of his power and protection spreading through me. Before I can say anything else, the pack is there with Jay at the front. One look at the scene, and he's beside us. I take a step back as they treat Jefferson. His healing powers are stronger than that of an average wolf, and I know he'll be okay, but I still feel guilty for what he did. I should've been more careful. I should've known better than to try and help a lone wolf. He was only looking out for

himself and wasn't going to risk his life for ours. Now Jefferson is hurt because he protected me.

But looking out for the unlucky is exactly what Jefferson taught me to do. I watch as the wolves gather round him, and I realize that this is the last time I'll have someone watching my back. When I go back to my pack—back to Rylan—I will be alone. Just like that lone wolf.

CHAPTER 2

*T*he forest opens up around me with mind-bending clarity. I can feel every grain of dirt beneath me, every blade of grass brushing against my body. The air is filled with smells and sensations of the forest. The colors are nearly blinding in their vibrancy, merging together into one giant masterpiece. My paws connect with the cool earth, as the birds chirp overhead. The combination of sights and sounds surround me in their comfort. It's not only the feel of the forest that tugs at my heart. It's also an otherworldly connection. This forest is my *home*. Longing presses into my chest as I think of leaving it.

Maybe I should've stayed at the village, but once again, I need to feel this land around me, before I am no longer part of it. Jefferson has recovered within a day, even though he'll carry the shoulder pain for a little longer. And we'll be leaving within hours.

I race over the soil. My speed is faster than that of an average wolf. Since shifter blood rushes through my veins, I'm anything but average.

I am a girl. I am a wolf. We are one.

This can't be happening.

Panic rises inside my limbs. The reality of what's happening slams into me like choppy waves crashing against an ocean shore. This is not something I can escape. It's not something I have control over.

When I finally stop my frantic race through the forest, I don't shift back to my human form right away. Standing at the edge of the cliff, I look over the tops of the trees and the darkening blue sky and simply breathe it in. Everything about my life is about to change. Again. And I don't know if I'm ready for it.

That voice in my head, I can still hear it echoing. It was a summons, directly from the alpha of my home pack. The pack that exiled me. I am still bound by the rules of that pack, whether I like it or not. I have no choice but to obey. It's that cut and dry. Alpha commands, the wolf obeys.

Regardless of how I feel about the alpha.

My senses pick up a small movement before my ears do. A wolfish smell comes next. I don't turn around as my current alpha, Jefferson, steps out of the forest. Of course he followed me.

Shifting back into my human form, my dress re-material-izing with the shift, I take a seat at the rocky edge of the cliff, waiting for him.

Jefferson took me in all those years ago. He nearly raised

me. Yes, he knew my parents, but he didn't have to do this. He didn't have to save me. My exile never made sense to me, and I thought I'd never have to see those good-for-nothing wolves ever again. But here we are. Stupid, stupid fate.

"Trinity–"

All it takes is my name and the tears come. Jefferson has not only been my alpha, but he's also been like a father to me for almost seven years. I don't want to leave.

"I know you don't. But such is the way of our lives."

I don't have to say the words out loud. He can sense my emotions. I'm not sure why I'm trying to hide them in the first place.

"It's not fair," I say, glancing at him as he takes a seat beside me. He's also wearing clothes, a pair of jeans and a t-shirt. Most packs don't bother with modesty, but since we've been working closely with the Hawthorne witch coven, we've been trying not to shock them with our nudity every time we come into town for a meeting. Our magic has always allowed us to carry clothes on us, but we never did before. Not regularly at least. The witches helped spell our magic to preserve the integrity of our clothes, regulating the feel of them, so they're not uncomfortable. Our body temperature runs hotter than most creatures, so clothing adds an extra layer of discomfort. But wearing clothes is like second nature to me now, which is great since I love pretty dresses so much. But even if I didn't, I don't think I could ever go back to just running naked.

Especially not now that I'm going back to a pack that hates me. I will never feel free—or safe—again.

"Why do they even want me back?" I grumble, not

keeping the dismay from my voice. Jefferson can read my emotions, and if he wanted to, speak directly into my mind. But it's also Jefferson, and I trust him enough to be vulnerable in front of him. That's something wolves are not good at.

"You know I have the same amount of information as you." Jefferson studies me in that calm way of his, thinking through the words he wants to say. "When you go, when you follow this command, I need you to remember something. You are a strong woman and a strong wolf, Trinity. Don't ever forget that those two sides of you are important in equal parts."

I nod, more tears coming to my eyes. There are packs out there who adhere to the old ways of living, where the wolf is dominant and human ways are mostly forgotten. Those packs are wild and unpredictable to outsiders. Not nearly rabid, like lone wolves, but not really part of the world either. I think back to what I remember of my pack, and nothing but hatred returns. I wipe at the tears, meeting my alpha's eyes. Jefferson is the only creature alive who has ever seen me cry.

"What if I can't handle it? What if whatever is required of me is more than I can handle?" Voicing the doubts quiets my mind somehow. This is something Jefferson taught me when I first came to live with him and his mate. Keeping things bottled up will only drive me insane. So I find a safe place, and I let those things out. Both Jefferson and Jay have been that safe place for me. Lately, it has also been the witches. Now I'm giving it all up.

"Trinity, look at me."

It's not a command from an alpha, but a request from the man who raised me. I meet his eyes. The care I find there would've taken me to my knees if I weren't sitting down. "You have always been much stronger than you give yourself credit for. Never forget who you are or the principles you have learned here. And know that, whatever happens, you will always have a safe place here."

He reaches for me then, holding me close. I cling to him as if he could chase all my doubts away. After this moment, I can no longer show emotion. After I say goodbye to Jefferson's pack, I have to say goodbye to this life and to the person I've been here.

I have to become the version of myself I've been keeping at bay for years.

* * *

SAYING goodbye to the pack is much harder than I anticipated. They line up outside the den, somber looks on their faces. It takes everything in me not to cry. I'm not about to show weakness, even in front of this family. I have to keep my tough exterior on.

It's practice for what's to come.

But when I see Jay, I think I'm going to lose it, even before he makes a move. I hiccup over my tears as he steps forward, wrapping his arms around me. Tucked into him, I hold on for dear life.

I didn't want to say goodbye in our wolf form, because it felt too final. I thought I could handle it in human form much better. Clearly, that is not to be so. My tears are silent, but my body shakes.

"You are the strongest she-wolf around. Don't you ever forget who you are," Jay whispers as he hugs me tight.

When Jefferson took me in, Jay was the first to accept me. He's the closest thing to a brother I have, someone who's been my friend and my mentor in the way the others haven't. He knows about my past, what happened with my pack, and who I'm returning to. He understands my fear, even without me having to say it.

"You are pack, Trinity. You are family." There's force in his words and then the wolves move. They surround us as one, enveloping me in their midst, raising their heads to the sky in a howl. All pretense of strength leaves me as tears flow freely down my cheeks.

Even though wolves are strong on tradition and family values, they didn't have to accept me. They didn't have to care for me. But they did. In the most incredible way possible.

I stand in the midst of them, soaking it all up. Jay takes my forearm as I pull back, giving it a firm squeeze as the others move. I would be worried about him if he didn't have the most amazing girlfriend, Leah. She's one of the witches of Hawthorne. In the last few months, I've gotten to know her personally, and the experience has been incredibly eye opening.

Just like witches, shifters grow up with a particular prejudice when it comes to the other magical species. Witches and shifters have always coexisted but never interconnected. That is, until an Ancient evil began rising again, and we were forced to work together. Everything we knew about the magical world changed after that.

It's been a bit of a learning curve. Now I'll have even more to learn.

"I'll keep your room exactly as you left it," Jay says, still touching my arm. "I promise to keep my hands off the comics as well."

"Graphic novels, James. Graphic. Novels." I roll my eyes, and he chuckles, but even this moment has tension. I'm not taking anything with me as I go. I have no idea if my original pack is living in caves or in houses. There isn't a way to know which items of mine will be accepted and which will not. The only thing I have is the red mini dress I'm wearing. The ruffled bottom and the sweetheart neckline are coupled with tie bow straps and a row of buttons at the front. It's my favorite and one thing I'm not about to leave behind. Instead of boots, I have my white converse on. It's the most me outfit. In a way, it's my armor.

"Trinity, it's time."

Jefferson waits at the edge of the clearing, his kind eyes on me. He'll take me to the meeting spot. Since the Ancients roam the earth now, every precaution must be taken. Even though he's still recovering from his wound, he's not about to pass on this responsibility to anyone else.

There are so many things I wish I could say, but nothing seems appropriate. So, I give Jay another look, hoping he knows just how much he means to me, and then I turn away and shift.

Stepping into my wolf form is as easy as taking a breath. Many pups struggle with it still, but it's always been natural to me. Now, I pull on that comfort along with every other comfort I can find.

Whatever I thought my life would be, it's about to become a whole new ball game. And a lot more miserable.

Especially because I have to deal with Rylan again.

CHAPTER 3

*J*efferson and I travel through the forest in our
wolf forms, keeping our pace faster than usual.
We wouldn't want to be caught off guard in
these woods. Since we have no idea where—or even what—
the Ancients are, we must be diligent. Even after all this time,
we still know close to nothing.

After traveling for most of the day, Jefferson finally slows
down. He doesn't shift, so I don't either.

"We'll sleep here tonight," he says in an alpha communication directly to me that doesn't require him to speak out
loud. I nod in understanding as he leads me to a collection of
boulders. They're piled high, but there is a smaller, circular
spot at the base with rocks surrounding the area from all
directions but one. The spot can be easily defended, even
though it's not a deep cave. I don't hesitate to step inside,
curling up against the rock wall, my eyes on Jefferson. He sits
closer to the entrance, his back to me.

I close my eyes, trusting him to keep watch. The trust that we put in our alpha is part automatic and part earned. Jefferson has always been the kind of alpha who deserves all respect. I can't imagine Rylan ever getting that kind of treatment from me.

"*Sleep, Trinity,*" Jefferson says without turning around. He can clearly feel my emotions getting riled up. "*Rest.*"

The tension I feel seeps away as I close my eyes and do just that.

It's the screaming that wakes me.

The birds' shouts of distress are nearly too much for my shifter hearing. I'm up on all fours before I'm fully awake. Glancing around the tiny cave, I see no trace of Jefferson. Fear grips my heart. I focus my breathing and open up my senses. He wouldn't have just left me, that much I know. There is danger somewhere beyond the safety of this small cave. I can tell that without the help of my magic.

The smart thing would be to stay here, but it would also keep me trapped. I'd rather have the forest to run into, if needed, than be pinned to these walls if someone finds me.

Stepping out of the tiny cave, I scan my immediate area, searching for Jefferson. It takes me a moment, but then I feel him. He's straight west, farther than I thought he would be. I pivot in his direction when his voice stops me.

"*No, Trinity. Stay away. Head north. I'll meet you there.*" His alpha powers allow him to speak to me, even across all this distance. I concentrate, trying to pinpoint his position.

"*What is it? I can help!*"

"*A creature. Similar to the one we encountered. Must investigate. Go!*"

The power of the alpha is behind that last word, and I have no choice but to obey. Frustration rushes over me, as my body turns and heads north, away from Jefferson. The birds cry overhead. There are enough of them that I can't tell where they're coming from. It's like they surround me on every side. Everything in me screams to turn around and go back, but I can't go against my alpha's command.

My mind races with all the possibilities.

The creature could be anything. The Ancients experimented with magic. That's how the first shifters came about. In reality, it could be anything or anyone and Jefferson is all alone against it. Already injured from saving me. Now he's doing it again. He's been like a father to me. He stepped in when no one wanted me. I can't just leave him.

I can't.

I stop running, my wolf vibrates with adrenaline, but she doesn't push forward. I stand alone in the middle of the forest, my heart nearly beating out of my chest. The command still resounds in my mind, but I'm no longer controlled by it. Even though Jefferson isn't my prime alpha, his powers became binding the moment he took me in. Turning slowly, I look back in the direction I came from, confused how I was able to stop running. I think if I wanted to go back, I could. Just the fact that I can have that thought stuns me. What does this mean? Is Jefferson...alive?

Jumbled thoughts full of panic rush through me as I think of worst-case scenarios.

The sound of movement reaches me, and before I can react, Jefferson bursts through the trees. All the fight goes out of me as I stare at him, while confusion pulsates inside of me.

"*You stopped,*" Jefferson says. All I can do is stare. He doesn't seem surprised, and it wasn't a question. I don't know what to say because I disobeyed a direct command. I didn't even think that was possible. As I continue to process, Jefferson nudges me with his nose.

"*Let's get moving. We have a ways to go.*"

He seems unharmed, besides his earlier injury. He's clearly ready to be away from here and whatever creature he left behind. He also doesn't seem to want to talk about what happened with me. I can't fault him for it. Tucking that away to examine later, I nod, and just like that, we're running once again.

* * *

WE REACH the meeting spot in the middle of the next day. I still have questions about what happened back there, but it doesn't feel like the right time to ask them. Jefferson has been on full alert, and it's not my place to question an alpha regarding anything. When we finally slow down, I realize we're near a town. Jefferson shifts into his human form, and I follow suit.

He motions for me to follow, and we step out of the woods behind a diner. Glancing around, I try to find anything that looks familiar, but I've got nothing. This town isn't near my pack. Jefferson leads me inside, and we take a seat at a booth.

"Where are we? I don't know this town," I say after the waitress brings us glasses of water and we drink them in full. While we can live off the land, nothing beats a cool glass of water and some air conditioning. I'm a girl wolf that likes her amenities, clearly.

"This is just the midpoint. A neutral meeting spot."

"Why all the cloak and dagger?" I look out the window, keeping my voice as controlled as possible. I'd be lying if I said I wasn't nervous. But no one needs to know that.

"It was the requirement."

I want to ask a ton of questions because Jefferson spoke to the other alpha. We do actually still use cell phones when it's convenient for us. They had a very clipped conversation, and I only heard one side of it. Okay, I eavesdropped. No one can blame me. But I can't seem to bring up the questions. Maybe I'm still hoping all of this is a bad dream and I'll be waking up from it soon.

"What did you see in the woods?" I decide to change the subject. It seems much safer to do so.

"I'm not sure, Trinity. It was not a creature I've come in contact with before. I couldn't get a read on it."

"But you saw it."

"Not exactly."

My brow furrows in confusion as I try to understand. Jefferson was right there, how could he not have seen?

"It might be a magical defense mechanism, not being able to be fully seen. It almost—"

"What?"

"It almost seemed to shift in and out of existence. Like

22

those superheroes with clocking abilities you like to read about. Similar to the creature we met a few days ago, yet different at the same time. It's—alarming."

That puts it mildly.

"Which direction was it moving?" Of course that's my next question. I'd beg Jefferson to head back immediately if I thought the pack was in trouble.

"East. Don't worry yourself, Trinity. We'll be okay."

I know they will. The community that Jefferson and Meredith, the coven's leader of Hawthorne, have created is the safest place for anyone, even though the town is so close to the epicenter of the Ancients' rising. But from what I've heard, Hawthorne isn't the only town with a power nexus under it. So, there are plenty of towns and epicenters of rising to be worried about.

I'm about to ask more questions when everything inside of me stills. A complete and total awareness fills my senses. It's like I can feel him before I see him. Turning, I watch as the door to the diner opens, and Rylan steps inside.

My first impression of him after six years is that he really grew into those boyish looks of his. Close to six-five, his dark hair is a little too long, falling into his eyes. The black t-shirt he's wearing pulls tightly across his muscles, the jeans sculpting his thighs. His jaw could cut diamonds, and his eyes are as piercing as ever. They're midnight blue and fixed entirely on me. Awareness slams into me with the intensity of his gaze. The feeling of seeing him again coupled with my shifter senses opening back up to his pack are nearly over-whelming.

For six years, I couldn't feel them at all. The wolves who were supposed to be my family. Now that the awareness of them is back, suddenly and without preamble, I'm drowning in it—and in Rylan—all at once. He smirks, as if he can see my emotions. I raise my chin a little higher. I will fake it until I make it if it comes down to that.

Jefferson stands to greet him and the two wolves behind him while I stay seated. I know Jefferson isn't exactly pleased by my sign of rebellion already, but he also gives me a knowing look, as if he expected it.

"Jefferson, we appreciate you delivering our Trinity back to us." Rylan's voice is deep and rich, and like fine wine, it has gotten better with age. The way my name sounds on his lips should be illegal. If I had even an ounce less of self control, there would be an outward reaction. Instead, I demand my body to stay absolutely still and don't allow any kind of visible discomfort to show. My wolf is even more aggravated. I wonder how long I can keep her at bay.

"I have to admit, I was very surprised when I received your summons," Jefferson says.

"There is a situation that requires Trinity to be home."

I snicker at the word *home*, and four pairs of eyes turn on me. I haven't paid much attention to the other two wolves that came in with Rylan, but now I take a second look. Even after all these years, I recognize them immediately. Ezra and Zachary. They're Rylan's shadows and best friends. Once upon a time, I was part of their group too. Both stand at about six-three, Ezra has curly brown hair and brown eyes. Zachary is as blond as if he spends all of his time in the sun. While Ezra watches me with no emotion on his face,

Zachary's amber eyes actually look like he might be slightly happy to see me. It makes sense. From what I remember, Zach was the fun one, who was way more in tune with his emotions than the others. But even so, neither make a move to acknowledge me beyond the stare.

"Jeez, I know I look good, but can you cut it out with the staring? I'll let you take a picture later," I say, as I pick up my empty water glass and put it back down. I could swear Jefferson is trying not to smile and that makes my heart a little lighter. "Also, you just pulled me out of my *home* to come here." I wave my hand around. "So let's skip the pleasantries and get on with it."

Rylan's gaze has turned even harder, while I talked, but I'm not backing down. We might've been best friends once, but all of that changed the moment he betrayed me. I'm not even going to try to pretend I've forgiven him.

Because I haven't.

"You're here because this is where you're needed," Rylan says, speaking in the vicinity of me, but not actually to me. I slide out of the booth, making him take a step back. He really is so much taller than me, but that's not about to deter me. His eyes flash with something I can't quite identify as he takes all of me in for the first time. I don't miss the way his eyes flicker over my body, head to toe, with an efficiency I can only assign to Rylan. His gaze leaves a heated imprint on my skin, and I have to work to keep myself still.

"Let's not talk about my needs, shall we. Just tell me what you want, and we can get on with it."

We're close enough that I can feel heat radiating off his body. He's not moving. Neither am I. This brings back a

25

million memories and emotions I don't want to deal with right now. When I don't budge, Rylan sighs.

"The pack needs your help."

My eyes narrow, because the way he says that, it almost sounds like the pack needs my help and my help *only*.

"I'm going to need more than that."

CHAPTER 4

*W*e leave the diner behind, heading for the woods. I know Jefferson needs to leave, but he's just as curious as I am. Once we're past the tree line, away from the prying eyes of the public, we stop. The locals were having too much fun gawking at the shifters. It's probably because they're so tall, and no other reason whatsoever. I swear my wolf just laughed at me. Sometimes, she finds me hilarious. Rolling my eyes, I focus on the wolves in front of me.

"How is it that you need *my* help?" I ask, folding my arms across my chest. Rylan doesn't answer right away, giving me a thorough study with his eyes. Again. It takes much of my self control not to fidget under that scrutiny. Or feel other— inappropriate things. Maybe I should just punch him in the face. Then, at least, he wouldn't be so pretty.

"Are you done?" I snap. His eyes fly up to meet mine. They hold me captive for a split second. I feel the gaze in my very core. I think he's going to call me out on the disrespect. Instead, he looks at Jefferson.

"Shifters are going missing from our home." Rylan's words slam right into my heart. "We've been tracking the disappearances for months and haven't been able to find even one missing wolf."

There's silence as that sinks in.

"How do you think Trinity can help?" Jefferson asks, glancing over at me. He's being protective, and while I appreciate the gesture, it only reminds me that he has to leave and I have to stay. My heart hurts for those missing shifters, but I have no idea how this involves me.

Rylan glances around again, as if he is searching for an answer in the trees. When he turns his attention back to us, there's something in his eyes I can't quite read.

I used to be able to. When we were kids, I could anticipate his actions before he even thought of them.

Squashing down that momentary trip through memory lane, I hold Rylan's gaze, daring him to speak. He stares back just as intensely. A million unspoken words hang in the space between us.

Rylan is the first to back down, shifting his gaze to Jefferson, who hasn't missed a thing. I try not to fidget under his inquisitive gaze, keeping my eyes on Rylan instead.

"The Oracle has advised us on the matter and Trinity is vital to resolving the situation."

His features pinch, as if it pains him to say the words. I'd comment on his reaction, except my mind buzzes with his confession.

"The Oracle?" I manage. My thoughts race through all the information I know about the creature.

From my limited knowledge of the Oracle, which isn't much, is that she is the final say when it comes to the politics of the pack. While the alpha is the ultimate leader, the Oracle leads even him. She has a specific kind of sight. It's not something I understand, even after spending time with the witches. I know the alphas have a hierarchy of Elders, and the Oracle overrides even them. I've never met the Oracle of this region. For a while, I was angry about that. Back when everything went down, she could've kept me from being exiled. But she didn't.

"She sent a request for my presence, and when I arrived, she provided me with information regarding the missing wolves. The main point was in regard to Trinity."

It doesn't go unnoticed that he's not addressing me directly, only talking about me to Jefferson. The urge to punch him in the face swells up again. I wonder how many times I'll have to squash that particular bug.

"Can she really be trusted?" I ask, and four pairs of eyes turn in my direction once more.

"Trinity, you know how these things work," Jefferson says, using his soothing voice. I throw him a quick smile, knowing exactly what he's doing.

"Let me rephrase that then," I say, turning back to Rylan, "Can *you* really be trusted? Who's to say you didn't bring me here to use me in some sick game?"

"Trin—"

"No, Jefferson. I think it's a very reasonable question," I interrupt, holding up my hand. Ezra and Zach are at Rylan's back, but I can tell they're on high alert at the display of my aggression. I didn't even realize I was this riled up, but I feel it now. My wolf and I are ready for a fight, if it comes down to it.

"Rylan here has done nothing but manipulate my life for his own purposes for as long as I've known him. Am I really to believe that he's not doing so now?" I give Rylan a sweet smile, watching his jaw clench.

"It doesn't matter what you believe." He growls.

"Oh look at that, you finally acknowledged my presence." I can't help it, everything about him antagonizes me. The impulse to shift and attack is nearly overwhelming. My wolf is right at the surface, ready to come out and play.

We're back to staring, as if there's only the two of us in the whole world. His next words are softer, missing some of the anger from before.

"You've changed."

His words nearly disarm me, but I've spent the last six years building up walls. They're not about to crumble.

"Yes. Being exiled and abandoned by the people I cared about does that to a wolf." My words are hard, my eyes on him. If I wasn't staring him down, I probably would've missed the tiny twitch of his eye, but it doesn't matter anyway. He can feel whatever way he wants regarding the situation. I know it was his fault I got kicked out. I'm not about to forget that.

"Now, if what you've said is true, I'm still not taking your word for it. I demand to see the Oracle. I demand to speak to her myself. That seems reasonable, no?" That last part is directed at Jefferson. As I turn to him, there's a bit of pride in his eyes. I can tell he's trying not to smile. I've always had that effect on him. The pain of knowing he has to leave returns in a burst.

"I believe that is a reasonable request and should be honored," Jefferson says, turning to face Rylan. The two alphas stare at each other, but I already know the answer. Rylan is going to let me see the Oracle, because for some reason, he needs me here. And he knows I'd become a lone wolf before I return to the pack of my own volition. So, when he speaks, I'm not surprised.

"Fine. We'll go see the Oracle."

SAYING goodbye to Jefferson is nearly impossible. Even though I knew the time was coming, it still hits me like a ton of bricks. He hugs me tight, letting me know in that one motion just how much I mean to him and his pack. Tears threaten to come, but I push them back. I'm not about to let Rylan see me cry.

"You are going to be just fine." Jefferson speaks directly into my mind, so the others can't hear him. He's not their alpha. *"It will be hard, but you are strong and smart. Trust your instincts. Especially when it comes to him. Don't ever forget who you are."*

He's said that to me before. It's a reminder I will now carry with me. Stepping back, he gives the wolves a quick once over before he shifts. After one last look at me, and he turns and runs into the woods. Every wish I have goes into hoping that he makes it home safely. Then the gravity of the situation hits me.

Once again in my life, I am all alone.

Yes, logically I know there are three burly wolf shifters right at my back. But they are not family, and they are not friends. When I turn to face them, I make sure my walls are higher than the Tower of Babel.

Ezra and Zachary haven't said a word, but I can feel their gazes on me. Are they waiting for me to snap or something? Who knows what kind of lies Rylan has fed them over the years. I narrow my eyes at them before I turn attention to their alpha. He stands a few feet in front of them, his eyes already on me.

There's no trace of the boy I knew when I was a young pup, no warmth or laughter on his face. It's like we didn't share our childhood, didn't share our secrets, our fears, our dreams. Didn't spend days laying by the Quarrel's Pond, laughing until our stomachs hurt. He's a stranger. Completely and entirely a stranger.

"If you're looking for a way to kill me, I won't go down without a fight," I say, placing my hands on my hips. My words seem to shake him from his strange stupor. He turns to the wolves. They nod at whatever he says to them, and I'm annoyed and glad at the same time. Annoyed that I can't hear what he says, but also glad, because that means his alpha powers haven't transferred onto me yet. I'm still connected to Jefferson, and I'm going to hold onto that for as long as I can.

Ezra leaves without a word as Rylan takes out a phone.

"Really?" I nod at the device in his hand, and he only shrugs as he turns away. That leaves me with Zachary.

"Are you going to tie me up and carry me over your shoulder if I misbehave?" I ask.

He chuckles. "As fun as that'd be, I'd like to keep my limbs attached to my body." Zachary comes to stand nearer to me. He's not as tall as Rylan but just as big. Although, there's something about him that just makes me think "teddy bear," not that I'd tell him that. Actually, I've met bear shifters before, and they're not cuddly.

"You think I can take you?" I ask, looking up.

"I most definitely do," he replies, grinning down at me. For just one second, I feel a connection. It's probably just my wolf looking for companionship, but it's nice. Even if it's fleeting.

"Ezra is ready. Let's go."

Rylan comes back over to where we're standing, gives us a look, and then keeps walking past. Rolling my eyes, I follow. I expect us to shift and head into the woods, but when we round the corner of the building, Ezra is there with a truck.

"You guys are just full of surprises, aren't you?" I say as Zachary opens the door and motions me inside. Even though I want to argue and ask a bunch of questions, I get in without a word. If I'm honest with myself, I'm exhausted. Emotionally more than anything, but also, that was a very fast trek across hundreds of miles. Jefferson and I didn't exactly rest either. I don't trust these guys enough to sleep, but at the same time, what are they going to do? Push me out of a moving vehicle?

That would actually be an option...if they wanted to mess

with me. But since they need my help—at least for now—I think I'm safe from that.

The moment Rylan is behind the wheel, Ezra is in the passenger seat, and Zach is settled next to me. I lean my head against the window and shut my eyes.

Wherever we're going, at least I can ignore them if I'm sleeping. It's as good a plan as any right now. My survival skills are really kicking in here.

I nearly laugh out loud at the irony of calling them survival skills when I'm actually ignoring all my instincts by taking a nap. But before I can even manage a laugh, the heaviness settles over me, and I fall into dreamland.

CHAPTER 5

*I*t's been years since I've dreamed this particular dream, but I know immediately where I am. My subconsciousness opens up to the unwelcome intrusion, but the emotions are there. I have no control over them.

I'm in a dark space with no ceiling and no floor. There's water, but I somehow stand on top of it. No matter how hard I try to move, I can't. I'm attached to this one spot, surrounded by complete darkness.

And then, the voices come.

It's not only that I'm bombarded by cries for help mixed with shouts of agony. It's that I feel each and every emotion that follows them.

My body vibrates from shock, as if I'm absorbing each dagger of pain and misery into me. There's no time to process or even protect myself from any of it.

I open my own mouth to scream, begging for a reprieve. But there's nothing. Nothing but darkness and pain.

The wolf inside me howls, the echoes of it bouncing off the space around me. There's no way out. No hope. Only the screams of the dying. My body shakes. My wolf and my human side are both in equal distress. And I can do nothing to stop it.

"Trinity!"

Someone shouts my name. My face snaps up, searching for where the sound came from. I hear it again and again, until it's the only thing echoing. Then I'm pulled out of there.

The first thing I see when I open my eyes is Rylan's midnight blue ones. He's only a few inches away from me, his face fills my vision. I can feel his voice all over me, and I realize he must've used his alpha command to get through to me. That's when I also notice his hands are on my shoulders. He seems to be holding me in place.

I pull back, just barely, and he drops his hands. When I nearly tumble forward, his hands return to my shoulders. I jerk away, righting myself. I'm still in the back of the truck, but now I'm at the edge of the open truck bed where Rylan holds me up. We've pulled up to the side of the road. From what I can see, there are trees on either side of the highway.

"What happened?" I ask, sliding out of the truck fully, if only to portray some kind of normalcy.

"What happened is you were throwing out emotions so strong I nearly drove off the road. Want to explain to us what that was?"

I glance behind him at Ezra and Zach. Both look slightly spooked and a whole lot concerned. I've never projected the dream onto anyone else before, not even Jefferson's pack. But I don't exactly want to explain in front of them either.

"I'm not here to air out my dirty laundry in front of an audience," I say, turning my attention back to Rylan. His eyes flash, just as ready to argue with me as I am with him. He's staring me down, probably waiting for me to cave. But I've spent six years building up my tolerance with building blocks of hatred and resentment. I'm not budging.

Rylan seems to realize that. He clearly says something to the other two because they shift and disappear into the forest, leaving Rylan and I alone.

"Fine, then tell me."

He's back in my personal space, my back hitting the truck as I take a tiny step back so I can keep looking at him. He really is giant next to me. That's only another thing I find annoying.

"It's none of your business," I snap, holding my ground.

"It's my business when you make my wolves shake in their seats, nearly forcing them to shift."

"What?" At that, I nearly move forward before I catch myself.

"Whatever was going on, your emotions—" Rylan stops, moving back and running his hand through his hair. "I felt it. My wolf felt it, and it was—a lot. I had to use my alpha command to get through to you."

The feeling I got at the sound of my name now makes sense. It was different than with Jefferson, but there was power behind it. I didn't like it.

Also, I don't remember Rylan ever looking unbalanced. But right now, as he turns toward me, that's exactly what I see. Clearly, the strange emotional attack I've been experiencing in my dreams seeped into the real world. I can't remember that ever happening before. Sharing the dream feels vulnerable, but I don't think I have a choice.

"It's a dream," I say, resigned. Rylan turns toward me, his eyes latching onto mine. The intensity of his gaze is too much. Maybe I'm being a coward, but I move my gaze over his shoulder to the woods beyond.

"It's always the same. A dark abyss. I can't move. And then I get—assaulted by screams and emotions, and it's nearly impossible to withstand. But there's absolutely nothing I can do. It starts and ends on its own."

Rylan doesn't speak immediately, mulling over my words. "You've had it before?"

"Yes. Not for a few years now, but it used to be frequent."

"And you have no idea what it means?"

"I don't know. The end of the world?" I throw my hands up in the air, moving away from the truck just so I can pace. I feel Rylan's eyes on me, but I can't look at him. "Look at the time we're living in. My past. The present. It's probably just my brain trying to process."

I fling the words at him unconsciously, but when he once again doesn't speak up, I turn to find him studying me. There's something in his eyes, but it's gone before I can pinpoint it. Not that it matters anyway. He may feel slightly guilty—or something—about exiling me, but he still did it.

"It felt like more than just a dream," Rylan says, which stops my pacing. I turn to face him once more. His eyebrows twitch. "I can't explain it, but we shouldn't have been able to feel it the way we did. It disturbed my wolf."

That is nearly unheard of. He's the alpha. Nothing should

be able to touch his wolf. We're back to staring at each other, and in this moment, I wish I could read his mind. Just for a few minutes, so I could know what he thinks of me.

If he thought of me while I was gone.

No. I close my eyes and turn away, suppressing that train of thought before it can take off. I'm not doing this to myself. When I was first exiled, I thought of him a lot. I wondered if he hurt as much as I did, and if he'd come get me. I wondered if all of it was a misunderstanding, and I'd be home with him soon. But that never happened. And I stopped expecting it pretty early on. I'm not about to let those thoughts back in.

"Where did Ezra and Zach go?" I ask, desperate to change the subject. We're not going to get any answers right now anyway. Maybe it would've been smart to talk to the witches when I was back in Hawthorne, especially Jay's girlfriend, considering they just went through a whole adventure with shared dreams. But it's been so long since I've had one, I didn't even think to ask.

"Scouting ahead. We'll drive to the next town before we park the truck and head into the woods."

"I'm still shocked you drive a truck."

"It's a strategic move." I glance at him in question, and he shrugs. "With everything that's been going on, sometimes it's safer to be in a truck. And if we ever have to—transport anyone, we have a way."

I nod, but before I can ask more questions, Ezra and Zach return. They both look at me a little apprehensively, and I smile.

"Don't worry. I plan on staying awake."

"That's a good idea," Ezra comments, speaking his first words to me in years before he heads to the truck. That almost sounded like a joke, but I know better. Ezra has always been the serious one. Zach on the other hand, sends me a friendly wink and I grin. They're keeping their distance for sure, but at least I'm learning their personalities all over again. I might as well, considering I have to live with all of them.

Glancing at Rylan I find him watching me again. I raise one eyebrow, before I walk back over to the truck. That conversation felt way too close to a heart to heart, and I'm not about to be having those with someone I hate.

* * *

WE REACH THE TOWN, but it can barely even be called that. The one Main Street looks straight out of a postcard. The rest of the town is mostly given over to the forest. Rylan seems to know exactly where he's going as he drives past the shops and parks in an alley behind one of the buildings. There's an overhead hanger here, and the truck fits perfectly inside.

"Come here often?" I ask as we get out of the truck.

"There are a bunch of towns in the area that are used by us," Zach says, coming around the back of the truck to stand next to me.

"Since when are you chummy with the neighbors?"

"While we don't work with the locals directly, in most cases, money gets things done, ya know?" He shrugs and I nod.

"I do know."

Zach opens his mouth once again, but one glance over my head, and he stops. I turn to glare at Rylan because he's the one shutting Zach up. I don't need to hear his alpha voice in my head to know. I roll my eyes but don't comment.

"What now?"

"Now, we eat. And then head south."

He doesn't wait for agreement, just turns and walks toward the end of the alley. I expect Ezra to follow, but he stays behind me. While Zach stays even closer. Great. I have bodyguards, apparently. I'd be offended, but I'm kind of honored. Rylan doesn't trust me, and he actually thinks I need to be watched. There's definitely a compliment in there somewhere.

I smirk, receiving a confused look from Ezra, but if he's going to be the tall and silent type, then I can follow suit. Well, with the silence. Not the height. It would be hilarious if I towered over them. The image does make me smile. At that moment, Rylan decides to glance back, and our eyes meet. I raise both eyebrows, challenging him without words. I swear I can see that I'm getting under his skin.

He leads the way to a diner on the other side of the street. Much like the last one we were at, this one has the standard booths near the window, and a counter for the more on-the-go customers. Rylan leads the way to the corner, sitting down first in the booth so his back is to the wall and he can see the whole restaurant from his vantage point. It's the exact seat I would've picked, and now I'm annoyed I have to sit with my back to the restaurant. Zach takes the seat next to Rylan. I slide in with Ezra beside me.

"This is cozy," I comment just as a waitress comes over. The guys order their food without looking at the menu, knowing exactly what they want. Clearly, they're frequent visitors. I opt for a burger and fries because it seems the easiest.

It feels strange being in a restaurant like this, acting like everything is normal. Last time I was in one where I actually sat and ate was at Whitney's cafe in Hawthorne. She makes some of the best baked goods I've ever had. It's where Jay took me when I was finally allowed to go into town. It's where he met his girlfriend, a witch who also became a friend to me.

Pain comes uninvited, much like pain always does. I miss them already, and I haven't even been gone a week. After my exile, I never thought I'd feel accepted anywhere. But Jefferson's pack made me feel like one of their own. It's not something I'll just get over simply because I'm strong and I'm supposed to. Jefferson has taught me that feeling emotions is an important part of *being*. It pertains to being a human and a wolf. Even though I know I will never feel comfortable sharing those parts of myself with the current company, I still need to be able to process it all.

If I don't, it'll fester inside me and end up destroying the me I've worked so hard to become.

The food arrives then, and I realize the guys haven't said a word. Well, probably not out loud. This whole disconnect between us is kind of getting to me now, but I'm not about to mention it. When Ezra perks up in his seat, however, I notice.

"What is it?" I ask around a bite of fries. When no one

answers, I put my food down and stare the two wolves in front of me down. Zach is the first one to look away. "Well?"

"Ezra is listening."

That makes me glance at the wolf beside me, but I don't comment. As a rule, when we're around humans, we mute our supernatural hearing as much as possible. It's a protective mechanism we learn at an early age. It helps not to feel overwhelmed when being around big groups of people. It's so automatic that I don't even have to think about it now.

It makes sense that they would be listening though, considering everything that's been going on. I still have very little information about what exactly is going on. There hasn't been a time for me to ask. We reached town too fast after our unplanned stop.

I can't exactly ask questions now either. Rylan is almost hyper focused on Ezra. He must have some kind of skill I'm not aware of, because any of us should be able to listen just fine. Frankly, we probably look crazy to anyone who might glance over here. We're just four people sitting at a table in silence, staring at each other. I try to catch Rylan's attention, but of course, he's back to barely looking at me.

My foot seems to have a mind of its own when it kicks Rylan under the table. All three wolves turn to me as one, shock on their faces.

"Can you guys at least pretend to be normal? You look like lunatics, sitting here in silence." I take a bite of my burger while they continue to stare. "Yes, exactly like that. The opposite of what I'm asking." I shake my head as I chew.

"You kicked me." Rylan's voice is full of—something. It

probably wouldn't be a good idea to laugh right now, but I want to.

"You're very observant," I reply after swallowing.

"You kicked me."

Now, I roll my eyes. "Did I hit a nerve attached to your brain and break it? We've established this already."

The growl that emits from Rylan travels over my skin, sending goosebumps all over. I fight to appear unaffected. It's not like I'm scared of him, even though I probably should be.

Actually, it's interesting that I'm not. But I'll think on that later.

"I know you're trying to look inconspicuous," I say slowly, as if they don't understand my language. "But you're three giant males sitting in a booth in complete silence, staring at customers. They're about to call the cops on you. So act normal."

Rylan is still glaring daggers at me, but my words must reach him on some level because he leans back in his seat a little, at least trying to look less imposing. Not that he's succeeding.

"How do you know so much about—this?" Ezra asks. And wow, he can address me without looking like he's about throw up. We're making progress?

"Jefferson made sure I know how to live in 'polite society.'" I use the air quotes because it always made me laugh when he called it that. Sadness flares up again, but I push it away. "You guys clearly don't get out much."

"We do what we have to," Rylan says, his voice hard.

"And right now," I lean forward, lowering my voice, "that

means not looking like a group of serial killers that has come to town. So chill."

I know I'm not making any friends here. Challenging Rylan on every level is not going to earn me any points. But I don't care. If I have to suffer through this, so does he.

CHAPTER 6

We leave the diner behind and head down Main Street, away from the truck. I can tell the guys have been talking without letting me in on their conversation again. Now I'd like to do more than lightly kick Rylan under the table. He's driving me mad, and he's not even doing anything. It's simply his presence.

"You mind sharing with the class?" I call out when I can't take it anymore. "What did you hear back there?"

"It's not your concern."

"Excuse me?" I stop in my tracks, making Zach and Ezra stop as well. Rylan takes a few more steps before he realizes we're not following. We're nearly on the outskirts of town now. It's even smaller than I thought.

"Move."

"No."

We're staring at each other with about ten feet between us, yet it still feels like he's right in front of me. I can feel the two wolves at my back, but of course, they stay out of this.

Before I know what he's doing, Rylan moves. His alpha speed makes him nearly a blur as he grabs me, spinning me into the alley. Then we're face to face. Both of us breathing heavily. The hand he has holding me in place on my upper arm is nearly scorching. I'm trapped between the wall and his body, but I'm not scared.

"You will show me respect. I am your alpha." He growls, and I can see his wolf in his eyes. He's near a shift, letting his wolf out just enough to be menacing.

I don't even blink as I glare up at him.

"You are not my alpha, and you will never be." My voice is low and dangerous, and I enunciate every word. My own wolf rises to the surface, picking up the challenge he's putting down.

"I am the alpha of this pack. You must obey."

We're both breathing heavily, our bodies shaking with nearly unrestrained rage. But I am not a pup who will be bullied around any longer. My power comes from knowing who I am, and I am a strong woman and a strong wolf. Jefferson has raised me to never minimize myself around anyone. I'm not about to start now. So I raise my body toward Rylan, bringing our chests flush together as I stare up at him.

"I don't obey. I don't respect. I won't be bowing down to your powers. You don't control me. Better get that through your thick scull now. You have to earn respect. And you have threw every possibility of that away when you threw me away."

47

My words ring out around us as if I've shouted them from the mountain tops. Our breathing, still heavy, seems to sync as I exhale into him, and then he inhales and vice versa. The sensation is strange and otherworldly, our chests moving as one, but I won't be the first to move away. He brought me back. Now he has to deal with me being here.

"You've changed."

He said this before, and just like then, the words hit me hard. Because I have. When we were best friends, I was still tough, but I was hopeful. There's none of that left in me now. Once again, I've been separated from my home, from people who care about me. From my pack. I'm not here to make things easy for him.

"Deal with it," I say, and then, I do slip away. It feels a little bit like giving in to him, but I can't handle his proximity any longer. He drops his arm, letting me move. His scent surrounds me, seeping into my pores. I'll carry it around with me from now on.

"I need more information on what's happening to the wolves," I continue, keeping my voice firm. "I need to know where we're going and how we're getting there. And I need you to speak to me when you speak to Zach and Ezra. No more of that direct alpha secret stuff."

Rylan doesn't reply right away. I doubt anyone has ever talked to him like this. I'm acting like his alpha, instead of the other way around.

"Is that all?" he finally asks.

I raise one eyebrow. "For now."

There's a moment where I think he might actually crack a smile. It's almost a glimpse of the old Rylan, the wolf who was my best friend. If I was different, I'd almost hope it was true. But that's another thing I don't believe in anymore —miracles.

* * *

No one says anything as we rejoin the others. Clearly, they heard the exchange. They didn't even have to be supernatural beings to do it. We weren't quiet. But they don't comment, and surprisingly, neither does Rylan. I know I pushed him back there. I'll have to be a bit more strategic about when and how I do it next. That was a gamble. It paid off, but I know it won't always work.

When we reach the forest, Rylan stops, turning to me.

"Here's what we know. Wolves are going missing. Never more than one at a time. There's no rhyme or reason to when or where. They're gone and aren't seen again until—"

"Until?"

"Until they attack." This is new information, and I furrow my brow.

"I thought you said they're never seen again."

"They're not in—their natural state." He stops, taking a deep breath. "They're almost rabid with no control over their shift. The few we encountered, they wouldn't shift back. They were—wild wolves."

I don't know what to do with that information. It slams straight into my heart, gripping it in fear and sympathy. A wild wolf is even worse than a lone wolf. My own wolf is right at the surface, just as distraught. A wolf without the capability to shift is a prisoner in their own body. It's absolute torture.

"Why didn't you say so before?"

"We didn't need other packs to know."

"You mean Jefferson. Why not? He has a whole coven of witches at his disposal. He could provide us with a way to find answers."

"No!" There's that alpha voice again. I stare at Rylan, waiting for him to go on. "This is a problem we can handle."

"Oh yes, you've been doing a great job so far."

Rylan growls, but I'm not fazed.

"Why not go for help?" I glance at Ezra and Zach, but they won't meet my eye. "Rylan?"

I think that's the first time I've said his name out loud. It stops me, just like it stops him. We stare at each other. Awareness creeps over my skin, sending pleasant goosebumps all over.

Pleasant?

Shaking my head, I push it all away. "Well?"

"We don't know who to trust." He clears his throat, raising his chin a little.

"You mean other packs. You think other packs are involved?"

"We don't know. But I'm not willing to take the risk."

My mind is spinning with so many thoughts, I don't even know where to start. If there are wolves out there, losing their ability to shift, that means it's a direct attack on shifters. Whatever is happening might not have anything to do with the Ancients, which is the default answer to all the wrongs in the world right now. But maybe not this time. Not if Rylan thinks other packs are involved.

"How do I fit into the picture?" I ask. He doesn't answer right away, and I take a step forward. "Rylan."

Because I'm watching him, I see the power his name has over him. Coming from me. I try not to overthink that, but he meets my eyes then, and I know he can tell that I can tell. He doesn't like it.

This strange web we've been caught in is going to destroy us if we don't find some kind of escape. But I have no idea how to do so, or how to navigate while trapped.

All I feel is trapped.

"Why am I here?" I ask again. This time, he does reply.

"I don't know."

It looks physically painful for him to utter those words. That is pretty normal for an alpha, but even more normal for him. Rylan was a proud wolf, even before he took the mantel of Alpha. I know it wasn't his choice, at least not back then. His father, the alpha of the pack, disappeared right along with my own parents when they were summoned by the Elders. They either never arrived or never returned. We could never figure out what happened. So Rylan inherited his father's place before he was ready. Before it was time.

Then, everything went to hell, and I was exiled.

My heart hardens before it can find any sympathy. I'm not here to hold Rylan's hand while he figures this out. But I can't go against the Oracle, not if what she says is true and if I can help. I would never want a wolf to suffer. Not if there is something I could do about it.

"How long has this been going on?" I push for more answers, since he seems to be in the talking mood.

"Five months."

"And you only summoned me now?"

"I only found out about you now." Rylan turns away, clearly ready to be done with the conversation. "We need to move. It will be dark soon and I want a good place to rest. We have a lot of ground left to cover."

Then, without waiting for a response, he shifts. My breath catches at the back of my throat at the sheer size of him. He's larger than any wolf I've ever seen, as white as freshly fallen snow. His midnight blue eyes are a stark contrast against his fur. Outside of this pack, I've never met another white wolf. I was always an anomaly in Jefferson's pack, as most of his wolves were brown and grey.

But here stands a reminder that I come from this pack, that White Wolf is my heritage. Rylan watches me as I study him, and I can't even imagine what's going through his mind. Shaking my head, I pull myself together and then I shift.

My wolf is also large, but still smaller than Zach's and Ezra's. They stay by my side, silent, but watching. I wonder what they think about all this, about their alpha bringing me back—being unsure.

It doesn't matter if I'm being honest. This is nothing more than a job to me. I'm here to do it and then, hopefully, I can return to the people who actually love me.

CHAPTER 7

*W*e fall into a routine. An annoying and frustrating—as well as mostly silent—routine. Staying in our wolf forms for the majority of the trip, we hunt for our own food, take shifts staying on patrol when others rest, and don't talk about anything.

Zach and Ezra seem to be used to Rylan's stoic mood. Maybe he's always this shut down. That's the best way I can describe him right now. Anger brims under the surface of his skin, sure, but it's like he's put up his own force field, pushing everything—and everyone—out. I should know. I've perfected that move ages ago.

A part of me thinks this is a game. Or a challenge. How long will I last if I'm given the silent treatment? Little do they know, I can go for as long as I need to. My stubborness can rival Rylan's, any day.

Two days later he finally breaks. At least, I'm calling it that and giving myself a point.

"The town is on the other side of the next meadow," Rylan says in our heads, as we get settled for the night. *"It'll be half a day's trip. We'll stay there and do some recon."*

I know he's mostly talking to Zach and Ezra, but he's finally decided to include me in the pack link. Not sure what that is about recon, but they know this area better than I do. I don't think I've been on this side of the country since I was exiled, so I have no recollection.

I show no outward acknowledgment of his inclusion while I find a tree to rest against. It's been two days since I've shifted, and a part of me wants to do it now. It's been years since I've stayed a wolf this long without letting my limbs stretch out. As the guys settle around in a perimeter, I decide now is as good a time as any.

Shifting, right here on the ground, I stretch out, my dress pooling at my upper thighs. The bow has come loose over my right shoulder, so I reach for it, tightening it up as I sit.

That's when I notice all three of the wolves are now in their human form, staring at me. Rylan's eyes draw me in, hot and pointed. I fight my body's response to it. Standing slowly, I keep my gaze on him, raising one eyebrow in challenge.

"You see something you like?" My words are barely a whisper, but he seems to visibly jerk before narrowing a glare at me. He doesn't like being called out in front of his pack. Well, too bad. Zach and Ezra look away, but they're just as invested in this as I am. I'd like to push more of Rylan's buttons.

"You and those ridiculous dresses. I see you haven't grown out of that habit."

Oh, so he's going on the defensive. That's okay, I can play this game as well. I let my hands linger over the straps before I run them slowly down my body, smoothing the material against my skin. I like the feel of it, the ruffle at the bottom of the skirt. Letting my lips curl at the side, I look up at Rylan.

"What's wrong with my dress?" I'm all sugar with that question, keeping my head slightly down and my gaze up. It's almost comical how Rylan's brain seems to short-circuit.

"It's—well—a dress."

"I don't see a problem." I cock my head to the side as Rylan narrows his eyes. He knows what I'm doing, and he doesn't like it. Well, I can see he's not immune to my charms, and therefore, I assume he hates it.

"It's impractical," he finally says. I can't keep a straight face anymore. I roll my eyes, straightening my shoulders.

"So is everything you're saying, but that doesn't seem to stop you."

Zach tries to swallow a chuckle that turns into a cough when Rylan spins around to glare at him. I can almost feel his alpha power radiate as he stares down his beta. Surprisingly, Zach doesn't cower and that kind of makes me feel better about the whole dynamic. Rylan doesn't say a word, simply storms off into the woods, leaving us in the small clearing. I shrug and go back to stretching.

"Why do you wear dresses?"

The question surprises me, and I glance up to find Ezra studying me carefully. I stand up straight, pushing my hair back.

"Because I love them," I reply, shrugging a little. "They

make me feel pretty and carefree and more like myself. Kind of like my wolf does."

I have no idea what possesses me to answer truthfully, but the words are out before I can stop them. Maybe it's simply because Ezra seems to actually be interested. He himself wears clothing that's different from the others. A buttoned down shirt and slacks, versus the t-shirts and jeans the others favor. While I was angry with the whole pack for a while, Rylan is the only one truly at fault. He's the one I've hated for six years. The rest of them were just following his command. Maybe if I can push my bitterness and anger aside, I'll see that not all of the pack is bad.

But the moment I think that I set it aside. I can't be getting soft now. Once I start, there's no going back. I'll unravel and there is no way I'm letting Rylan see me like that.

I don't wait for Ezra to comment further, but I think he might actually be thinking over my words. I move back to the tree I found and shift into my wolf form. Laying down, I curl into myself, closing my eyes. Sure, traveling this fast and hard is exhausting. But so is the array of emotions that keep rushing through me. What I wouldn't give to be able to talk to Jay about it, to be heard and seen and cared about. Just for a moment.

I almost snicker out loud. Why wish for things that will never be again? Focusing on my anger, I cleanse myself of all sad thoughts and finally relax enough to sleep.

* * *

WE MOVE EARLY the next morning. The sun isn't even fully up yet. All four of us are on high alert, as if there is a sense of danger in the air that we can't quite reach. But we're ready.

At least we thought we were. But nothing could prepare me for the horror I see when we hear that first growl.

"Don't let them bite you," Rylan shouts straight into our minds. *"Protect Trinity."*

His command wasn't meant for me, I can tell. But it surprises me. That surprise costs me.

A dark brown wolf jumps out of the bushes to my right, aiming his teeth straight at me. Instantly, I catalogue the wild animal in his eyes, the way saliva drips from his growling mouth. He reeks of decay, a walking corpse. I recoil immediately, jumping to the side so he barely misses me.

In my training, I've fought as a human and as a wolf, but this opponent is something different.

"If we don't want them biting us, I assume we don't bite them?" I yell, making the wolves flinch. It's the first time I've spoken to them through the link which Rylan clearly left open.

"No, don't bite."

"Then how do I fight them?" I ask, jumping out of the way once more. This is completely pointless. We'll keep playing this game until one of us wears out. And I think that one might be me, because this wolf seems to have energy on a whole other plane of existence. I glance at my companions. They're being pushed back by three other wolves. Four on four. I guess, at least, the odds are even. With that thought comes another one, but I don't have time to grab it before the wolf leaps again.

I get an idea then. There is something I can do. It's going

to hurt me, on a deep level, but I don't see another choice. My eyes dart to Rylan. I see the others doing the same dance I am, except they're using their heads to butt the decaying wolves, throwing them against the tree trunks. It doesn't help. The rabid wolves are on their feet even before they fully hit the tree. They're too wild, too far gone to feel any pain.

I concentrate on the one in front of me, trying to speak to it in my wolf form. There is nothing but static in the other wolf's head. I can't even sense thought of any kind.

A howl breaks out across the clearing, and I jerk my attention toward the guys. Zach is now pinned under two of them. Rylan and Ezra both throw their bodies at the other wolves, trying to tear at their flesh with their claws. The other wolves don't hesitate to answer in kind. When a claw stabs right through Rylan's skin, he roars, grabbing the wolf by the throat and throwing him across the clearing. The wolf flies straight into a broken branch, getting impaled on it with the force of the toss.

All of this happens in mere seconds, and then the rabid wolf is upon me. Instead of moving away, I welcome the impact, shifting at the last possible moment. I hear my name vibrating off of my skin, but I don't have time to hesitate. Reaching for the knife strapped to my upper thigh, I yank it out and slice it right across the wolves throat as it towers over me.

With superhuman speed, I roll out of the way, just as blood gushes out and the wolf drops down, nearly crushing me. Crouching low to the ground, I'm ready to spring forward for another attack. Instead, the two remaining wolves seem to freeze for a second and then they turn and race back into the woods.

Okay, another weird thing to add to the growing list.

I don't have time to think on that right now. The grunts of pain coming from Rylan are enough to jumpstart me into action. I race across the small meadow, sliding to my knees next to him. He's covered in blood, but I can't see where he's hurt through the fur.

"Shift." He doesn't seem to hear me as he tries to get to his feet. "Rylan, *shift!*" I snap, this time my voice a little louder. Rylan stops, staring at me for a moment before he shifts. He drops onto his back with a thud.

"You're bossy," he mumbles.

"And you're delirious." I check his shoulder. It is snapped nearly completely off with far too much of his flesh showing. I need to bind it, and then I need to get him to shift back to heal.

"Ezra, find me some bandages. Zach, I need water. Preferably hot." The two, still in their wolf forms, stare at me as if I've lost my mind. "What? You speak human. Go! He needs this."

That snaps them into action or maybe Rylan said something to them directly. I don't know and I don't care. I may not like Rylan, but I swore to help the wolves if I could. This, sadly, includes him.

"Don't do me any favors," he growls, as if he can read my mind.

"Don't flatter yourself. This has nothing to do with you," I say, before I push—hard—on the wound. His scream of pain should bring a smile to my face, but it doesn't. He squirms under my touch. It would really be more helpful if he was unconscious right now.

"Hold still," I say, grabbing the bottom of his shirt and yanking it so a piece tears off. Now I can see his stomach, and I'm suddenly distracted. Someone's stomach should not look like a work of art. Shaking my head, I turn back to the task at hand and find Rylan's eyes on me. There's a glimmer of cockiness in them, so when I push down on the wound, I do it extra hard. He squirms even more, nearly fighting me off now.

"I said hold still. I need to get as much of that wolf's blood off and out of you as I can."

"It won't help if I bleed to death," he snaps, his words barely audible through the grinding of his teeth. He jerks away when I reach for him, so I do the only thing I can think of. Swinging my leg over that finely defined stomach, I straddle him with my thighs. He stops moving immediately.

The spot where his skin touches mine is a furnace. That one little space on my body could probably warm a village for a year now. I want to pull back, but he's finally still enough for me to wind the piece of fabric around his upper arm. Hopefully it will prevent any more of the blood from traveling down. I'm not a doctor. I have no idea if I'm doing this correctly, but this is the only knowledge I've got.

Ezra returns first, a first aid kit in his teeth. He freezes at the sight of me straddling his alpha, but now is not the time. I wave him forward just as Zach returns. He gives me the same look, but moves forward without prompting. He dumps a thermos at my side before both of the wolves shift back. Zach opens his mouth, but I send a glare his way.

"Come over here and hold him down. I have to clean the wound." The wolves move as one. All thought of pleasantness leaves as they hold their alpha down, and I pour hot water over his wound.

He's not going to forgive me for this one.

CHAPTER 8

*W*e're close enough to the town that Zach and Ezra could carry Rylan there. But there's no way that's happening. He's too proud for any kind of help and having his betas display strength above his is unspeakable.

I know all this because I understand alphas. Once upon a time, I understood Rylan. Not much has changed.

I'm on the other side of the clearing, giving him as much space as possible. He's weak, but he finally shifted, so the healing should go much faster now. He growls any time Ezra or Zach walk up to check on him. Clearly, he's not in a fine mood.

While they're all occupied, I slip into the woods, heading in the direction the wolves took off in. Somehow, while we were busy helping Rylan, the two fallen wolves disappeared. I have a feeling the others came back and carried them off. Now, I'm following what little of the tracks and scent I can find. When I feel a wolf behind me, I'm not even a little bit surprised.

"Your turn to babysit me?" I ask, without turning around. There's a moment of silence and then Zach sighs. I can tell it's him by his scent. Each of them carries their own unique identifiers. Zach's is more freshly opened leaves on a tree waking up in spring from its winter slumber. Ezra is more woodsy, something like a lumberjack I would imagine.

Rylan...Rylan smells like a storm brewing. HIs scent is rolling clouds and electricity filling the air right before the first drop of rain. I push thoughts of him away as Zach speaks up.

"You can't be wandering off alone."

"I'm not alone." I turn and give him a quick grin, noticing how his eyebrows furrow in response.

"Trinity—"

"I just want to know we're safe. I need to see how far I can track them."

"You won't be able to."

That stops me. I turn to watch Zach shrug, waving his arm in front of him.

"Their tracks only ever go this far. It's like they disappear into thin air. We can't sense them and there are no visible markings to follow."

Looking around, I realize he's right. This is as far as it seems to go.

"Why do you think that is?" I ask, trying to push my senses out to make sure there's no one close by. All I find is Rylan and Ezra.

"We don't know. We can't seem to figure anything about these wolves or what's causing their behavior."

"It's not magic; that's for sure."

"What?"

I meet Zach's eyes, finding confusion there.

"Their magic, the part that makes them shift, it's missing. I can't tell if they're enchanted to stay wolves or if that part of them was ripped out. But it's gone."

Zach continues to stare at me as if I've lost my mind. But I know what I felt, what my wolf felt. There was no connection between us on that level. It was like trying to read a blank slate. There was nothing but empty space there.

"How can you tell?" Zach asks now, bringing my attention back.

"You can't?" He shakes his head and I narrow my eyes. "What do you sense from them?"

"Just wolf. Nothing else."

"Like you would a normal wolf? An animal?"

"Yes."

I glance around the clearing again, trying to work through that. Why would I sense them on a different level? Is that why the Oracle says I can help, because I have a different perspective? But Rylan should be able to feel them the way I do. His alpha bloodline is much stronger than mine. His father was an alpha, and now, so is he. So where is the disconnect? Because there definitely is one.

"We should head back," I say now, and Zach falls into step beside me. I thought I'd feel awkward with them always around, but already, I'm falling into a routine. And so are my senses. Zach feels familiar and friendly. I can't tell if it's because my wolf is desperate for connection or if it remembers the pup I played with as a youngling.

Either way, I push it away. I can't give into that feeling of friendship. I know all too well how fast it can be ripped away. Zach hasn't re-earned the place of friend yet. Or a packmate. We're just doing our duty at this point, both of us.

My wolf whines a little at my thoughts. I know she misses Jay. He's the one who would always go explore with me, the one who was always there to watch my back. Zach walking beside me in silence is too much of a reminder of that. I hate that a part of me wants to let my tears through.

But of course I won't. These wolves haven't earned the right to see my vulnerability. They never will.

When we step through the trees back into the clearing, Rylan's eyes are on us. He's still in his wolf form, but I can tell he's better. I have no idea what kind of poison—if any— the rabid wolves carry, but I'm hoping the Oracle will be able to check Rylan over. I'd feel—something if he keeled over on my watch.

"How far is the town? I should go investigate. Make sure none of the wolves went there," I say, brushing the bottom of my dress with my hands. When I glance up, Rylan's eyes are following the movement. I narrow my own, pulling my hands away and putting them on my hips.

"It's too dangerous to go on your own," Ezra says, glancing between Rylan and me.

"Great, then you can take me. I assume you guys are tag-teaming babysitting me?" I glance at Zach, and this time, he doesn't manage to hide his smile.

"No one is going anywhere."

"Well, dear *alpha*." I make sure to put emphasis on that word, but not the way he'd like it. "You're out of commission, and there are innocents in that town that need protection. If we're not too late already. Unless you'd like me to carry you in like a child, I'll go with my first plan."

I can feel anger radiating off him and toward me, but I'm not backing down. Right now, I have the advantage and I'm going to milk it for all it's worth.

"Ezra, go with her," the alpha finally says. The other wolf stands without preamble.

"See ya later, boys," I call over my shoulder, not waiting to see if Ezra follows. My heart slows down just a tad as I walk away from Rylan and his penetrating gaze. If I don't learn how to control my body's response to that look, we're all going to be in trouble.

* * *

THE MOMENT we reach the outskirts of town, I shift back. We find no tracks or any kind of indication that the wolves went this way, but since Zach pointed out their disappearance, I didn't think we would. Ezra has stayed beside me and silent the whole time. It's partially why I manipulated them a little to have Ezra come instead of Zach. Ezra doesn't actually want to talk to me.

We find an alley close to the forest and step into it. Coming out of the alley will be a lot less conspicuous than us appearing out of the forest. I keep waiting to hear some kind of noise of distress—screaming or shouting—but the town is operating as usual. I let my senses expand across the space, cataloguing the laughter and the chatter. A mother soothes a crying child on the other side of the park while a couple exchange loving words in the opposite direction. But everything is as it should be.

"So where did they go?" I mumble. I continue walking down the street with a silent Ezra beside me. But then, he finally speaks.

"What is it that you are trying to find?"

I sneak a peek at him, but his eyes are forward, scanning the immediate area. I shrug anyway, rolling my shoulders a little.

"Mostly, I wanted to make sure there isn't any carnage. We should probably also get some food, since we won't be making it into town today."

Ezra nods, and I can almost see the gears turning in his brain as he processes.

While they do a lot of things I didn't expect them to, like carry clothes into their shift, these wolves still seem very unlearned in the way of humans. It makes me wonder about the way they live. I probably should wait to ask someone who may be a little better at talking, but Ezra is all I got right now. I'm too curious to wait.

"Back with the pack," I begin. I can tell his attention zeros in on me, even though he still continues to watch our surroundings. "What type of environment is it? Do you live in your wolf form for the majority of the time?"

Since we've been traveling so fast and staying in our wolf forms, it's an understandable question. There are packs who only turn human once every few months or less. Sure, I have my memories to guide me, but that doesn't really mean anything anymore. A lot can change in six years.

"We still live in the village," Ezra responds, his answer clipped.

The words bring up an image of a clearing, surrounded by some of the tallest trees I've ever seen, with small houses built in between them. There are caves nearby as well, close enough to be considered part of the area.

"Are the wolves given a choice?"

Some packs require a shift or no shift, but others, like Jefferson's pack, are given a choice. Part of why my relationship with my wolf is so symbiotic is because I've never had to suppress her or myself. I didn't even consider it might be different here. While Ezra takes his sweet time replying, I nearly run out of air.

"Yes. You are given a choice." I exhale at his words and so does my wolf. At least in that regard, I'll get to stay true to myself. I'll need some new dresses at some point, but that will be a problem for another day.

"You really don't remember...the pack?" Ezra's question takes me by surprise. He's not the one to initiate conversation usually. I glance at him as we reach the diner. He pulls the door open to let a family walk out before he motions me in.

"I remember." I decide on the truth. There's no use trying to keep secrets. "But everything is clouded in betrayal. So, forgive me if I'm not too trusting when it comes to my own memories."

There's more bitterness in that statement than I'd like to admit I have in me, and Ezra doesn't miss a thing. Thankfully, he doesn't press. We order at the counter, and I let my eyes roam over the crowd as we wait.

The feel of this place, the small town and the tourists, remind me of Hawthorne. I glance down at the amethyst beaded bracelet I wear on my left wrist, tracing it lightly with my fingers. Jay's girlfriend and her friends took me in, made me part of their group. We made bracelets from beads made out of different crystals. It was the first time I've ever done anything like that, and it pains me that it was the last time as well.

Our order is called, and Ezra grabs the bags without hesitation. When I look up at him, I notice his eyes flicker down to the bracelet. I know he's curious about it. If Rylan doesn't understand my dresses, he really won't understand jewelry. Ezra wouldn't understand either.

Even though we're all wolf shifters, it feels like I've stepped into a completely different world. It has nothing to do with the rabid, untraceable wolves running around. Everything about this pack seems strange to me, as if I'm only now discovering my wolf heritage and learning it all for the first time. Even though I feel like a fish out of water, I need to make sure I don't look it. I don't need to be give Rylan and the rest of them any ammunition against me.

As I look both ways before crossing the street, my eyes land on a building to the west. I did a lot of research back in Hawthorne, and I wonder if a human library might be able to yield any information on these rabid wolves. I doubt it. Once again, I get that pang of awareness in my chest, like I'm missing something vital.

Pushing all those thoughts aside, I follow Ezra back the

way we came over to the alley that opens up to the forest. Right now, we just need to get Rylan back on his feet so we can reach the Oracle. Then we can get some answers. More and more I've been wondering why was I summoned back at all.

CHAPTER 9

*R*ylan looks nearly normal by the time we make it back. Without a word, Ezra delivers the food and we settle back into our silence. I can feel Rylan's eyes on me, but I'm not meeting his. My mind is too filled with questions.

The rabid wolves. The Oracle. My summons. There's something here that I'm missing and I don't know if Rylan can give me the answers I search for. He might not be capable, but I also think he'd keep it to himself just to spite me. I can't trust anything he says, considering his go to when it comes to me is manipulation.

My eyes drift in his direction briefly, and I catch him staring. Instead of looking away, I cock my head to the side, holding his gaze. The electricity I feel when I'm near him crackles in the space between us, sending goosebumps over my skin. There's no way I'm looking away first, but then, neither is he. We'd spend the entire day staring at each other like this, and while I don't want to be the one to yield, I do anyway. Rolling my eyes for good measure, I lay back down on the ground, looking up at the trees.

The day has gone away already. The sun sets, making shadows dance at the tips of the tall trees.

It's never been easy to keep my memories at bay. I can't do so now, even as I try. My father and I used to run for miles, racing each other across the vast forest around our pack's village. And then, when we could run no longer, we'd shift and collapse onto our backs, staring up at the sky. Dad would tell me wild stories about realms where storybooks come to life and where fae are all kinds of different sizes. He wasn't the only storyteller though. He and Mom shared that particular trait. Their bond was unlike anything I've ever encountered when it comes to packs. There was genuine love and respect between them, not like a lot of the arranged marriages that still happen within packs.

That's one of the lessons I learned living with Jefferson. There are packs out there who stand by the old ways— arranged marriages and minimal shifting or interaction with the human world. Then there are packs who are more wild. Their bonds lie within their packs, their traditions set to uphold the old ways of life.

Not Jefferson's pack. He opened up his mind and adapted to a new generation. His own son is marrying a witch, something the old guard would never have allowed.

My heart fills with sorrow as I think of my parents and how much they would've loved to know this side of the pack life. Not the Ancients rising—a fact that we will always have to live with from now on—but the changes in the pack mentality. Our core values are still there, but they are even stronger now than before. It's a world my parents would've loved.

Of course, all of that could just be Jefferson. I have no idea how my old pack actually operates. Although, from watching Rylan with Ezra and Zach, I can see there's mutual respect there. I can't say I trust my own judgement, but I know that's stubbornness talking. And my own hurt.

Rylan may be fair to his betas, but he's never been fair to me. When my parents—and his father—disappeared, he could've helped me. Instead, he put all the blame on me and voted me out of the pack. The witches would say "voted me off the island" based on a popular show the humans watch.

There goes another layer of hurt, missing the witches and that part of my life that I just barely discovered. It seems that anytime I finally think I've found some kind of footing, Rylan is there to sweep the leg from under me.

He did it when I was eleven. And he did it again six years later.

I close my eyes against the pain, pushing it all away. It's completely pointless to dwell on the past or the hurt of missing my parents and my adoptive family. The only part of my past that I want to hold onto is the anger. It fuels me, like logs added to a fire.

Nothing stops me from burning hot, and I want to keep the flames high enough that no one can pass. I know I've let my guard down a little around Zach and Ezra. I can't allow that any more than I can allow Rylan to affect me in any way. As far as my life is concerned, everything is a business transaction.

If I can help the wolves somehow, then I will. But that's as far as it goes.

It's strange that I have to remind myself of these things when it comes to them—mostly just the betas though. I have no problem holding onto my anger when it comes to Rylan.

Turning on my side, I inhale the scent of the forest around me, the ground beneath me. I nearly groan when Rylan's scent reaches me as well. Annoyed at him for existing and vexing me so, I shift, curling into myself for comfort.

My own self is all I'll ever have, and that is more than enough. Closing my eyes, I force the tension out of my joints and sleep.

* * *

THE NEXT MORNING, we make it into town with no issues. Rylan is walking like he wasn't ever nearly torn apart by rabid wolves, but he hasn't bothered to say thank you. Not that I expected it. I'm simply keeping a running list of all the things the alpha owes me.

My life back is at the top of that list.

Ezra went ahead to scout, and Zach has been keeping a close eye on me. I was kidding when I said they were baby-sitting me, but now I truly believe Rylan doesn't trust me on my own.

I'm getting increasingly more annoyed with the alpha the more time I spend with him. Granted, I already hate his guts. But this is a new level. He refused to talk to me, expecting me to simply bow down to his wishes, and I'm so done with that.

When we pass a souvenir shop, I duck inside. I register Zach's surprised inhale as the door closes behind me. I find myself in a small shop, much like the one the eldest Hawthorne sister runs back in the town I came from. It's an herbal and crystal shop filled with all kinds of sparkly trinkets. The bracelet we made during one of our girl nights still adorns my wrist and I glance down at it fondly. Sadness reaches out to me again, threatening to pull me down. Before I can give in or get out, I'm grabbed from behind.

Spinning around, I'm yanked against Rylan's hard chest, the breath stolen from my lungs. His grip on my arm is punishing, but I won't let him see me flinch.

"What do you think you're doing?" His anger is barely contained within those words, which gives me the desire to smile. Provoking him has officially become my favorite pastime.

"Shopping, duh."

I go to move back, but he brings his other arm around my back, pinning me entirely against him. My dress and his t-shirt and jeans don't offer much protection against the feel of him. His muscles strain under the fabric, flexing a bit as he holds me in place.

One of my arms is pinned behind me where he holds it tightly. Our breaths seem to sync, with him inhaling when I exhale, and vice versa. We're one body operating on two sides yet together. Everything about this—about him—feels right and wrong at the same time.

When I finally narrow my gaze on his, I find him already watching me. The world has already fallen into a different dimension as we stand here, but now, my sole focus is him.

"You are testing my patience," he whispers, the rumble in his chest sending pleasant vibrations over my body.

"Didn't know you had any to begin with," I reply, keeping my voice as light and unaffected as possible.

When Rylan growls, I feel it in every part of my being. Goosebumps follow the path the rumble has taken, and my traitorous body would melt like a puddle on this floor if he wasn't holding me so tightly.

"You must fall in line." The words are barely audible through his anger, and I can see his wolf right under the surface. It gives me immense pleasure knowing I've gotten this far under his skin while doing next to nothing. If I really put my mind to it, who knows what I could do.

I'm not sure how long we would've stood here like this if the nice older lady, who I assume owns the shop, didn't come up to us.

"Is there anything I can help you with?" she asks, looking at us with a knowing smile. That one look makes me push against Rylan because I don't want to know what she's thinking, seeing us like that.

Rylan opens his mouth, and I know for a fact he's about to be rude. I place a hand on his chest. He freezes under my touch.

"No, we're just browsing," I reply, giving the woman a small smile. Her eyes sparkle as she watches us for a moment before she nods.

"Well, if you need any special—specific crystals or herbs, I have a whole variety."

She spreads her arms out toward a shelf, and I see an assortment of rose quartz, jade, and garnet. I swallow my immediate response, but I can't help glancing down at the older lady as she gives me a tiny wink.

After spending time with the witches, I recognize love crystals when I see them. Thankfully, Rylan seems oblivious.

"Thank you," I say before I turn to the alpha and push him toward the exit. The woman moves on to the next group of customers as I try to get Rylan out the door. He stares at me in disbelief. I think he's ready to grab me again, but I push past him and waltz out the door. Zach is on the other side of it. I have no doubt he watched that whole exchange because he's not meeting my eye. Or Rylan's. I'm almost positive he's trying not to laugh.

It's obvious our little embrace looked more like a lover's hug than an enemy's battle of wills. My body seems to like that idea a little too much, which only fuels my disdain for Rylan. His stupid hot physique is getting my hormones all out of balance.

He's got a *stupid* handsome face. And *stupid* sexy arms. And a *stupid* muscular chest.

What is wrong with me?

I need to punch something. Preferably Rylan, but I can't even look at him right now. Instead, I storm down the street in the direction we were walking before I decided to play my game. I didn't realize I'm not the only one playing, and there are more players involved than I thought. Like my ridiculous response to the alpha, for example.

I will definitely need to be more careful.

CHAPTER 10

ithout sparing me a glance, Rylan takes off the moment we're back on the street, leaving me with Zach. I want to question him, but I think I might be pushing him a little too much. No, I take that back, I don't push him nearly enough. I'm not pushing any of them nearly enough.

Zach and I continue in silence, but I can feel the beta wanting to talk. Out of the three wolves I'm traveling with, Zach is definitely the talkative one. From what I remember of him, he always has been. Now, I wonder if I can use that to my advantage.

"So," I begin, slowing down just a tad, and putting a little bit of a smile on my lips.

"Don't even start," Zach groans before I can say anything else.

"I don't know what you mean."

"Of course not. And your female wiles won't work on me,

so don't get any ideas." Zach smirks, but there's no malice or annoyance in his voice. He's amused.

"What female wiles? I was only going to make conversation."

"Mhmm." Zach glances down at me, and I try not to grin too broadly. "Conversation that most likely will get me in trouble."

I shrug, twirling a little as I turn to continue walking. At least he's talking to me, I guess. The way this pack moves is slightly annoying. Mostly because I'm clearly not invited into their inner circle.

My pack.

I need to remember to call it my pack. Because that's what it is now. No matter how much I don't want that to be the truth. The sooner I get over it, the sooner I can learn how to rise above it. The circumstances may not be ideal, but it's nothing I can't handle. Right?

Right.

If I say it enough times, it must be true.

"You think all I do is cause trouble?"

"Yes. Absolutely. One hundred percent."

My laugh surprises both of us. Granted, it's more of a chuckle, but still. It's not something I thought I'd be capable of anytime soon. Not when it feels like my whole life has gone up on flames.

"I suppose there are worse things I can be," I reply, shrugging. That makes Zach grin. It feels strange, sharing this almost normal moment in time with a member of a pack that abandoned me.

When I was younger, back when I first came to live with

Jefferson, and Jay became the older brother I so desperately needed, I used to rage about this. Why couldn't the pack stand up to Rylan? Why didn't anyone go with me? Why was I so dispensable?Jay always listened, and then, when I was too tired to put words together into sentences, he'd gently remind me that the pack has no choice but to follow the lead of their alpha. There was nothing any of them could've done, no matter how much they might've wanted to. And then, he'd remind me that he was choosing to be there with me. I'd throw the words back at him then, saying that he was only around because Jefferson commanded it. Jay wouldn't react to my anger. He had more patience than anyone I know. He'll let me spew all my anger out, and then he'd tell me that the only command that Jefferson gave was that I am part of his pack. Every other decision, he left up to the pack members. It's not the same as what happened with Rylan.

Rylan made a decree—an unbreakable command—for me to be exiled and for the pack to forget I even existed. Just thinking about it scratches at the barely healed over scar in my chest. The anger I feel toward him rises up once more. I'm grateful for the memory. It'll keep me safe.

I shouldn't be getting this chummy with Zach. While he may not be my enemy like Rylan is, he's not my friend. I can't forget that. He seems to actually want to say more, but I keep walking, ignoring his imploring glances.

Instead, I search the groups of people, trying to pinpoint were Rylan and Ezra disappeared to. But no luck. Zach leads me to the corner of the main street park, leaning against the tree as he waits. Seeing no other choice, I begin to pace in front of him. When one of the passing families gives me a strange look, I realize that my pacing is more like prowling. I need to chill.

This part of following someone's lead is always frustrating but even more so when it's Rylan who's doing the leading. Finally fed up with the wait, I turn to Zach.

"What exactly are we doing?" He spares me a quick glance before looking back over my shoulder.

"Waiting."

"For what? The harvest to come in?" Zach gives me a weird look but doesn't comment. Great, he's turning into another Mr. Stoic. I don't think I can take more of that.

"Zach," I snap my fingers in front of his face. His eyes latch onto mine, a small growl escaping his lips. He's much taller than me, but I'm not intimidated. The moment he sees that, I think he gets even more agitated. That makes me want to grin even broader. It's official. I enjoy getting under their skin.

Before I can do anything else, however, a prickle of awareness reaches me, and I turn my attention to Rylan. He comes from our left, his jacket unzipped and a new shirt peeking out from underneath. It was smart of him to change so as not to scare off the locals, so maybe these wolves do have a little more to do with humans than I remember.

"We're heading into the woods as soon as Ezra gets here," Rylan announces, barely sparing me a glance. That is fine by me. I don't feel like having any unwanted reactions right now, and I know I will if he turns those eyes on me. But I still need to get my digs in.

"What? No five-start hotel stay for us? But I wanted a bath with bubbles." I add just the right amount of whine into my voice, which makes both of the wolves look at me like I've lost my mind.

"Ha, you guys are gullible," I say, running my hand over my dress to straighten it against the slight breeze. I don't miss the way Rylan's eyes follow the motion, but I don't comment either.

"Where did you disappear to anyway?"

"The Oracle isn't easy to find," Rylan replies, clearing his throat. I hide a smile. I'm definitely getting to him. "She has contacts that provide information as she sees fit. But she knows you're coming, so she's willing to do a face to face."

"Wow, lucky me."

This whole Oracle thing is not sitting right with me at all. While I was kidding about the bath, I kind of wish I wasn't. It would feel incredible to be fully human for an hour or so and completely forget about the ordeal that's become my life. I'm really hoping the Oracle will have some answers.

AFTER GETTING SOME FOOD, we head for the outskirts of town. Ezra joined us shortly after we sat down at the restaurant, and he has not looked happy since. There's definitely tension between him and Rylan. As I watch the two of them now, I can't help but think Ezra is at the edge of rebellion. Something must've happened when they were together. I glance over at Zach, but he doesn't show any signs that he's concerned, so maybe I'm simply projecting.

Because I'm concerned. About everything at this point.

Thankfully, no one pays us any attention as we head to

the neighborhood off Main Street. Here, the forest is in everyone's backyard, so it'll be easier to disappear. I know I was kidding about a bath earlier, but I kind of wish we could stop and get cleaned up. I could really use a new dress too. This poor thing is looking like it's seen better days. In truth, it has.

Sneaking to the back of one of the yards takes no time at all. The boys aren't talking. For some reason, I don't think they're simply shutting me out of pack communication. I think they're actually not talking, and the silence is quite disturbing. Whatever is going on, it's causing unrest and I don't like it.

Once we're a few feet inside the forest with the trees shielding us from view, Rylan stops, turning to the three of us.

"It's a two-day trip from here, at least. Since we have to move slow. We'll have to be careful and beware of traps. The Oracle isn't one to allow just anyone to waltz into her territory."

I glance between the guys, but Rylan's whole attention seems to be on me.

"The closer we get, the more time we'll have to spend in our human forms. She's not fond of our wolves."

"That seems—odd," I comment, but Rylan seems to not register my words.

"It probably would be best if we run as far as we can as wolves before we have to shift back. It might save us some time traveling."

I nod, getting ready to shift, but then Ezra and Zach take a step back out of the forest.

"You're not coming?" I ask the question in their general direction. They glance at me, but it's Rylan who replies.

"The Oracle only approved the two of us to her territory."

Then, without waiting for me, he shifts. It's hard not to react to his wolf, even though I've seen it enough to be immune. But I'm not. He's huge, gorgeous. The white of his fur shines with its own ever-present glow. My own wolf is eager to come out just at the sight of him. That makes me hold my shift a second longer, just so I can pretend I'm not affected.

I'm pretty sure Rylan misses nothing.

Turning back to the boys, I give them a little wave. "Don't miss me too much," I say before I shift.

My wolf is smaller than Rylan's but not by that much. It begs a question I wish I had an answer to because even though both Zach and Ezra are bigger than me as humans, their wolves are about the same size as my wolf. I should be much smaller.

But that's a problem for another day. Rylan is waiting for me by the trees, and then, before I can even blink, he's racing off into the shadows. My body reacts automatically, chasing after him.

The feel of dirt beneath my paws, the smell of the forest around me, it almost makes me forget where I am. And with whom.

Every forest has its own district feel. I can't explain it any other way. Sure, it also smells different, but there's an emotion it evokes that's particular to that specific forest. This one, even though it's the same one we came from before coming into town, it's as if it's a whole new forest. It's like this part of it carries with it more weight, more magic. It would be the perfect place for the Oracle to hide, if she placed spells all over the place.

While there are numerous Oracles who exist across the world, each responsible for counseling with specific packs, no one can actually explain to me where they come from or who they are. They're part of our world, and they seem to have always been. Their council is sought when our lives are at the brink of change.

It's tradition. It's law. It's the way things have always been.

It's the reason why Rylan listened to the Oracle in the first place, even though he wants nothing to do with me. Or have me anywhere near his pack.

But I don't trust him.

And therefore, I have to find out what the Oracle knows straight from the source. But this whole traveling through the woods with only Rylan for a companion is not exactly my favorite option. Without Ezra and Zach to act as buffers we might just murder each other.

CHAPTER 11

*W*e move through the forest for hours with minimal rest. Our bodies can handle a lot, and I'm proud to say that mine can handle more than usual because of all the training Jay put me through growing up.

A familiar pang of pain grows in my chest at the thought of him. I push it away because I have no time to dwell. Only to move.

When the sun sets and the moon is visible through the tops of trees, Rylan finally slows down. Even though we see just fine in the dark, we're both tired. Rest will do us some good.

Rylan leads us to a small collection of rocks in the midst of the forest. There's no cave inside as far as I can see, just a pile of boulders. But it'll help to have some kind of a protection at our backs while we sleep.

The alpha shifts without a word, heading toward one of the trees. I shift as well, stretching out my muscles as I watch him. He studies the tree in front of him before moving on to the next one. The third tree finally gives him whatever it is he's looking for. He pulls something out of his pocket, slamming it directly into the bark.

There's a moment of stillness and then water begins to trickle out. Rylan cups his hands under it, glancing over his shoulder at me.

"After you."

I don't hesitate to move forward, placing my own hands under the water, and taking a few sips. We take turns for a few moments until the water slows and then Rylan pulls the device back out.

"You travel with a spile in your pocket?" I ask, raising an eyebrow.

"Only in the spring or late winter," he replies, and it almost sounds like he's teasing. We've been taught to live off the land, so of course I know that's truly the only time to get water from trees, since the sap is high in water during those times. But the way Rylan says it, it sounds like he's joking with me and I have no idea what to do with that. It's too much like the Rylan of before.

That's how I think of him. The Rylan of Before and the Rylan in the After.

The Rylan of Before was my best friend. He was the one I went to with my thoughts and dreams, the one I ran through the trees with when the moon was high. The one who was my partner in crime.

The Rylan in the After is the hard man standing in front of me, an alpha with mounds of baggage on his shoulders and a hatred for me in his heart.

It's crazy to think they used to be the same man.

Ignoring the range of emotions inside of me, I carry on stretching out my human body as I walk over to the boulders. It's as good a spot as any to camp for the night. Rylan collects some of the water for later, layering some leaves together to create a makeshift bowl. It would be even better if we had dinner. When my stomach growls as if in agreement, I nearly laugh out loud.

Rylan—who never misses a thing—hears it, of course. Our eyes meet. He's still near the tree when his gaze drops to where I've placed my hand over my stomach, hoping to quiet the noise.

There's heat in that gaze that I don't quite understand, but I still respond to on some level. I have the sudden urge to run my hands over my dress, much like I did earlier, to see if Rylan's response will be the same.

But I don't get to make that decision when his eyes meet mine once more.

"Don't leave."

He doesn't wait for a response to his command before he shifts and disappears into the woods.

"Sure thing, bro," I call out, hoping my voice and the casual way I address him needles at him. "I'll be a good little wolf and stay right here."

The growl I hear from the shadows makes me grin.

"*Can I at least make a fire?*" I ask, hoping he's smart enough to keep the pack communication link open to me. There's a moment of silence where I think he's not, and then,

"*Yes.*"

Pretty sure that yes caused him physical pain. What a

drama wolf. I roll my eyes and set about collecting sticks and dried out leaves. It's still early enough in the spring that it will be cooler during the night, and if Rylan manages to bring back food, I'd like to cook it.

I'm a lady, after all.

Although, if I have to live off the land like a wolf, I am more than capable. That part is something my parents taught me. They—much like Jefferson—believed that the wolf and human parts of us must live in unity. Therefore, both sides of us had to be able to survive. And thrive. I knew how to hunt before I could fully walk as a human. Rylan was better than me at that as far as I remember.

There were times—no. I can't keep doing this myself. I can't be taking trips down memory lane or thinking about the pack I left behind. All those emotions must be on lockdown, or I will not survive this. I will not come out intact.

Starting a fire takes almost no time at all, even without a lighter or a fire witch.

Let's just say, I've always been a good student.

When Rylan returns, he's in his human form, and he's carrying two rabbits. While there are magical beings who can make themselves look like rabbits, I can tell these are just regular animals. It's the circle of life.

Rylan glances at the fire but doesn't offer any praise or thanks. Not that I thought he would. He cleans up the meat and places it on a makeshift rotary before settling down on the opposite side side of the fire from me.

The one thing I hate the most about all this is how none of it makes me uncomfortable. It's like he and I have simply fallen into our old roles, moving in sync around each other and working in tandem when required.

As I watch the meat cook, I honestly don't know what to do with that realization.

* * *

WHEN THE DREAM comes this time, I'm almost expecting it. I'm not sure if it's because I went to bed so highly emotionally wired, or if I actually felt it. Either way, when I open my eyes, I'm in the black void.

It's the only way I can describe the space and the feeling it evokes. I'm still rooted in place, with water right under the bottom of my feet. And just like always, there is nothing I can do to prepare myself for the pain that comes with the voices.

This time, however, they are louder, more so than they've ever been before. Shouts of agony and helplessness fill my ears and the space around me. The desire to drop to my knees and curl into myself is nearly overwhelming. Yet no matter how much I may try, I can't do anything.

I can't move. I can't shift. I can't shut out the pain.

Suddenly, a burning sensation spreads from my fingertips up my right arm. Looking down, I expect to see my arm on fire, but there's nothing. Only pain. I grit my teeth against the torture as the fire pulsates inside my skin. By some miracle, I'm able to move enough to raise my arm to my chest, cradling it with my other hand. Tears sting my eyes as I push the pain down and away. Focusing my breathing, I pull on every lesson I've ever learned on how to control one's body's response to such an assault.

As suddenly as it comes, it dissipates. Pulling my arm away from my chest I glance down, only to nearly pass out from the sight.

There, on the right side of my right wrist, directly under the thumb is a small white tattoo. It's a wolf howling into the sky with delicate lines drawn as an outline. Intentional lines run from the top of the wolf's head down its neck. There's no body in the tattoo, just a close-up of a wolf's head and neck. At the very bottom, the part where the chest begins, is a tiny white star.

I stare at the tattoo, frozen by shock and confusion.

I've seen it before, the year I turned thirteen. It came to me in a dream—this same dream—only it was on my other hand. I have no idea what it means or why it appeared, because when I woke up, it wasn't there. I haven't thought of it in years, or even remembered it until seeing it again.

Before I can think too much of it, the voices grow closer. My body shakes from the assault. I try to pull myself away, to pull myself together somehow, but there's nothing but pain, residual burning on my arm, and the thousand voices screaming their release into the void. The pressure becomes a physical weight as I try to move with no luck.

"Trinity!"

My eyes snap open, yanking me out of the dream. I find myself looking into Rylan's eyes. He's on top of me, his hands pinning mine over my head, his legs straddling me on either side. My breathing is heavy and fast as I work to calm myself.

The deeper I inhale, the slower my heartbeat becomes. That's when I register the feel of Rylan's hands on my wrists, the weight of him over my middle. There's a moment where my body responds against my will, almost arching up toward him before I squish it down.

I'm nearly vibrating from the proximity, feeling flushed all over. This is a moment in time that's going to be embedded in my memory against my will. He's breathing a little heavy as well, as if he too isn't as unaffected as we're both pretending to be. I have to find solid footing again. I have to remain in control.

"Mind getting off me?" I say, raising an eyebrow.

"Promise you won't hurt yourself?" he replies.

I scrunch my face in confusion. He swings his leg off of me, pulling me gently to a sitting position. That's when I realize he's gripping my right wrist. Glancing down, I see the blood first.

"What?"

"You were scratching off your skin," Rylan says before he gently uncurls his fingers from around my wrist. Right where the tattoo in my dream was, there are scratch marks deep enough that the blood is flowing.

"I need to stop the bleeding," Rylan continues, glancing around before he reaches for his t-shirt. This looks a little too familiar to me, and I stop him.

"Here." I raise my hip a little and move my dress in his direction. "Take the bottom off."

I place my left hand over the blood and get to my knees. Rylan watches me with an unreadable look in his eyes before he takes the bottom of my skirt between his hands.

"Not too much," I remind him, because the skirt is already short. His eyes fly up to mine and then he does something peculiar. Still watching me, he begins to lower his head. I hold my breath as I try to figure out what he's doing. But then he leans to the side and grabs the bottom of my skirt with his teeth. His lips barely graze my thigh and my whole being seems to come alive with that tiny touch.

Rylan's body is tense as he makes a precise tear with his teeth. Then he sits back up. His hands take the bottom of my skirt, more gently this time, and tug at the tear. He moves slowly, across my whole front, until he reaches the other side. His knuckles brush against my thigh, before he tears the strip down. The front of my skirt is about two inches shorter, and I think I've aged about ten years, holding my breath.

Without meeting my eye, Rylan reaches over, picking up the bowl of water he collected earlier. Pouring it over my skin, he scrubs the wound with the bottom of his shirt. His touch I more gentle than I could've imagined it to be, sending pleasant goosebumps over my skin, all thought of pain forgotten. He takes the strip of cloth next, binding my wound. His touch is so meticulous it becomes nearly soothing and I almost lean into it. My chest fills with an unfamiliar feeling as I watch Rylan's bent head over my wrist. He's slow and careful with his movements, this gentle alpha, an entirely different creature all of a sudden.

When he's done, he stays on his knees in front of me, and I don't know what to do or say as I take my hand back.

Finally, after what seems like an eternity, Rylan raises his eyes to meet mine. His are ablaze with a fire I don't want to name. I swallow, if only to do something. Rylan's eyes follow the movement of my throat, then they move up to my lips before settling on my eyes once more.

If one of us doesn't move right now, then we'll do something we can't come back from. I feel that as surely as I feel the dirt under my legs. The dirt that doesn't belong to my home or the forest that I love.

The moment that thought comes, I shut down. Pushing back, I get to my feet, severing the—connection. Giving myself space, I turn toward the fire. That's when Rylan's voice stops me.

"Tell me about the dream."

CHAPTER 12

*N*either one of us wants to go back to sleep. Rylan's demand hangs in the air between us, but I'm still trying to recover from—whatever that was between us, to even form coherent words.

My skin seems to buzz with an awareness I do not understand. Glancing down at my wrist, I watch the blood darken the red fabric. I must've nicked a vein because it's bleeding more than I think it should. Even so, I can already feel it closing up—healing—in that special way our bodies do with shifter magic. A part of me wants to shift. I tell myself it's because I'll heal faster, but I know it's because I want to hide from Rylan and whatever this is.

But I am not one to hide.

Instead, I take a deep breath and turn around. He's standing about five feet from me, arms crossed. He watches me with his Rylan intensity. Even as a young pup, he always had this air about him. It's his alpha power, I think. Back when we were friends, I made fun of him—good fun, naturally. Now, I don't know what to do with it, but I will not succumb to it like every other wolf.

So I raise my chin a little, square my shoulders, and watch him narrow his eyes. Okay, getting under his skin is *definitely* my favorite pastime.

"It's the same dream," I finally say, but he's already shaking his head before I finish.

"No, it was different."

"What do you mean?"

"I mean, I could—feel it. It was different. Tell me."

"Always so demanding." I'm not sure what I think about him feeling anything when it comes to me. Especially my dreams. Those seem extra private. But maybe that's just because mine have been extra painful.

I don't think I can really hide the truth from him either. Not if he's going to find out anyway.

"There was just something about it. It felt...*more* somehow. I'm not sure if that makes sense to you or not, but it was heavier, the pain bigger."

He's quiet for a moment as he processes that. Then he glances down at my wrist.

"And that?"

"I don't know. It was a mark I needed to get off my skin." That part is fuzzy, somehow, and no matter how much I concentrate, I can't seem to bring up a full image. Even though it's right there, under the surface. Maybe it's my brain trying to protect itself, or some magic doing it. Only a slight white outline flashes in front of my eyes, before it's gone again. I stare at the bandage and try not to think about the way Rylan's mouth grazed my thigh.

"They never make sense, okay?" I shrug, forcing my focus away from the weird sensations that thought inspired. "It was always about how helpless everything felt."

"How you felt?"

"No. I'm always channeling someone else. Multiple some-bodies. The only wolves that can do that are alphas, so it makes no sense why I would be able to do that in my dreams."

Rylan doesn't push, and I don't offer anything else up because I have nothing left. My whole life is spinning out of control, and now the dreams are just as haunted as reality. I don't know how to deal with all of this, only that I must.

No amount of wishing away this situation or hoping for a different life will change that this is my only one. Even as a child, I never wished for the unreachable. When my parents disappeared, when I was exiled, I took every punch with a raised chin. Dad would've said that I should've blocked. Jay would be disappointed in my form. But standing tall against adversity has always been my only defense. And for a while, it brought me a safe haven and a home.

Looking down, I trace the bracelet over my arm. It's a reminder that not everything is hopeless, that there is still goodness in the world, and I have survived everything thrown at me so far. I can survive Rylan.

* * *

WE MOVE IN SILENCE, the forest mostly still in the early hours of the morning. The sun isn't up yet, and we should've rested more, but we both knew we weren't going to. My wrist has healed over, but I can still feel the sting of the scratches, the burning of the mark. Logically, I understand it's simply my mind playing tricks, but I can't shake off the feeling that it means something. Something more.

I do a quick study of our surroundings and that nagging feeling returns. It feels like we've been traveling for miles, but everything around us has stayed the same.

"*I think we're going in circles,*" I call out, hoping Rylan has kept the pack link open. He glances behind him to meet my eye before slowing down.

"*Why do you say that?*"

"*Everything about this forest feels the same,*" I reply, opening up my shifter senses more. The ground beneath my paws, the smell of the leaves and the dew on the small patches of grass, it's all familiar. Then, another sensation enters.

"*Do you feel that?*" I ask, glancing around once more. I can tell Rylan feels it too. It's like a ripple underneath our skin, an uncomfortable kind of tug.

"*I was given instructions to travel directly south until we come across a sign we cannot ignore.*"

"*Those are some very helpful instructions.*"

Even in wolf form, I can tell Rylan narrows his eyes at my sarcasm. It's his fault he's forgotten how I can be. Sarcasm is the language I speak best.

"*The Oracle must protect herself in ways she sees fit,*" Rylan says, and I can hear his annoyance echoing inside of my mind. The words are something I have heard before. When my parents were summoned, before they disappeared. It's pack law.

"I get it, okay?" I say before nodding my head to let him know he can get back to leading the way. Everything about this is annoying. I'm ready to reach the Oracle already and at least get some answers. We need to know what's going on. That's priority number one. I'm not naive enough to think I'll get all my questions taken care of. But if we're going to be put on some weird quest or be tested by running around this forest for days, I will be frustrated. And snarky.

Rylan looks like he's about to say something. If I had eyebrows right now, I'd raise one at him. But he decides against it, turning to head south once more.

We're back to running in silence. I'm really hoping we find whatever that sign is soon.

It's another hour before the weird nagging feeling returns. This time, Rylan is the one to stop our progress.

"What is it?" I ask, when he starts to shake his head as if he's trying to shake something off. He doesn't reply right away, and I dare to take a step forward.

"Hey, what's going on?" I make my voice even more gentle, moving closer. He rears his head back. I jump away as he shifts without warning. Dropping on all fours, he breaths heavily.

I'm about to ask again, but then I feel it. My wolf is being pushed aside. No, not aside.

Inward.

She's leaving me with each passing breath. I try to hold onto her, but it's like a bandaid being ripped off, and suddenly, she's gone. I'm thrust into my own shift. I'm fully human as I blink, dropping down to the ground.

Rolling over to my back, I try to catch my breath as panic sets in. She's gone. My wolf is gone.

But wait, no. She's not gone. Just...caged?

"Trinity. Trinity!" Rylan's face is suddenly above me as he keeps repeating my name.

"I'm okay," I manage, pushing myself to a sitting position and turning to look at him kneeling beside me. "But my wolf..." How do I even explain it?

"Mine is gone too. Somewhere deep inside of me."

I guess I don't have to explain it. Rylan looks confused—almost hopeless, and I have the nearly overwhelming desire to reach for him. I curl my hands into the dirt instead, keeping my head as clear as possible. There's only one explanation I can think of.

"Is this the sign we've been looking for?"

Rylan shrugs in the most human way possible, and I nearly laugh out loud. He looks completely and entirely lost. It's that puppy look in his eyes that nearly undoes me. Here's one of the toughest alphas around, and he looks like he needs a hug.

I will not be swayed by this. If I repeat that statement as a mantra it's bound to work. I hope.

"It feels—strange," I say, slowly getting to my feet.

"It feels unnatural," Rylan replies curtly. He's right, of course. It does. My wolf is there but not quite. I try to reach her, I try to shift, but my limbs aren't listening. It makes me feel helpless, not that I'd admit that out loud.

"I thought you said the Oracle only didn't like the wolf."

"Well, apparently, it's more complicated than that," Rylan replies, a little too curtly for my taste.

"Did this happen last time?"

"No. Last time, the Oracle came to me."

That's a piece of information I wish I had earlier, but oh well. Rylan will keep his secrets, even when they're pointless ones.

"So what do we do now?" I say instead, hoping I sound more confident than I feel. To be frank, I feel like part of my soul is missing. I'd like to do a very unlike me thing and lay down in the dirt and cry. But once again, that is not me, so here I am. Rylan struggles as well. I can see it, even though he tries to appear unaffected. He uncrosses his arms and turns in the direction we were traveling.

"We walk."

CHAPTER 13

*H*aving my shifting ability taken away makes me rethink every little piece of knowledge I possess about the Oracle. True, we don't know that much to begin with—she likes her secrets. I've never met the Oracle who oversees Jefferson's pack, so I can't even judge her against other ones. Maybe all of them are eccentric in their own ways.

If I was back in Hawthorne, I'd ask one of the witches to look into the lore of the Oracles. Since becoming friends with them, I've rediscovered my love for learning. It's something I gave up when I was thrown out of my pack. I just didn't see the point. But then, Jay taught me, and so did his girlfriend, and here I am, thinking about libraries and books and research.

After another twenty minutes, Rylan stops. He's been quiet this whole walk. Even though I want to talk this through, I'm no longer privy to his thoughts. Or he to mine. Instead, I just panic on the inside. There's no way this is permanent, right? It can't be. I also don't feel rabid like those wolves were, so it can't be that.

"You have to stop thinking so loudly," Rylan says. I twist around to find him watching me.

"What is that supposed to mean?"

"It means I can feel your panic, and it's fueling my own, so I need you to knock it off."

First, I can't believe he actually admitted to such a weakness. An alpha is never allowed to feel such trivial thing such as panic. But I can't even focus on that before my annoyance rises.

"Well, excuse me for not taking into consideration your feelings on the matter." My voice drips with sarcasm. "I should absolutely be catering to your whims right now."

I roll my eyes because I know it bugs him. Just like my words do. He may not be in his wolf form, but he can still growl at me. I'm sure that look works on all his other wolves, but it definitely doesn't on me. It just makes me more prickly.

"That's not what I meant, and you know it," he snaps. But I'm not about to let him off that easily.

"Oh really? Then please do enlighten me. How else was I supposed to take that?"

He growls again. I realize we've moved toward each other without even realizing it. Only a few feet separate us now, but I can already feel the heat of his body reaching out toward me.

"It doesn't matter what I say, you have made up your mind already," he throws back at me and frankly, he's not wrong. He's not getting the benefit of the doubt from me.

"So you're not even going to present your argument?"

"I shouldn't have to. I am your alpha."

"Let me stop you right there, wolf." We're now inches apart, and I hate that he's so much taller than me. "We've been over this one, and my tune hasn't changed either. Since pack rules don't seem to apply to me, probably because you exiled me. I get to choose an alpha. And you have to earn my respect."

His whole body vibrates with rage—or something else I can't quite name—but I feel it all over my skin. It's like I'm the one channeling him now, and I'm getting bombarded with too many emotions to sort them out properly.

"Why do you have to be so difficult?" He asks it like a question, but it also sounds like a statement at the same time.

"Because difficult is what I do best."

We continue standing like that, a few inches apart, and he opens his mouth again, as if to argue some more.

"While this is incredibly entertaining..." An unexpected voice sneaks up on us. We jump apart as if we've been burned. Turning, we find ourselves face to face with a gorgeous woman, who looks to be in her early thirties at the most. For a second, I'm taken aback before it sinks in that of course she's not some elderly grandma. Oracles hold special power. Rylan appears subdued immediately. I've always wondered if Oracles had a power over alphas. That answers that. She waves a hand toward a tree beside her, and the bark shimmers.

"Ready to come inside?" she asks.

* * *

STEPPING into the tree trunk takes a little bit of faith, even though I've seen magic up close. But Rylan steps through without hesitation. I follow suit with the Oracle bringing up the rear.

Immediately, I have mixed feelings about her. I can't tell if it's simply because of my parents' disappearance or if it's something else. Rylan doesn't seem to have the same misgivings, but once again, I wonder if it's because she has some special power over him.

All my worries are forgotten when Rylan moves to the side, and I get a good look at where we are. It's a garden, the most beautiful one I have ever seen. Flowers grow all over the area with pathways woven in between. There are dozens of different kinds, anything form tulips to lavender to roses. Large trees line the meadow and disappear farther into the forest. There are flowers hanging down from the branches as well, almost like curtains. If I had to guess, the trees look like willows, except for the flowers hanging down from the branches along with the leaves. Cherry trees, something I didn't know grew in this part of the forest, are dispersed around as well. It looks like it should be messy, colors and scents growing with no rhyme or reason, but somehow, it looks peaceful and exactly as it should be.

"I see you like my garden." The Oracle comes around, giving me a gentle smile.

"Are we still in the forest?"

"We are and we are not."

Great. I've forgotten how much these magical types like their riddles. I think she can tell I'm holding back an eye roll, if her little smile is any indication.

"It is good to finally meet you, Trinity Whitewolf."

Her words nearly bring tears to my eyes. No one has called me by that name since the day I was exiled from the pack. It is used as a title, even more so than a name, a way to show that one belongs. I'm not sure why she's using it now.

It doesn't matter anyway. I raise my chin a little, meeting her eye. We came here for a reason, and I have a ton more questions than I started out with.

"Where is my wolf?" is the first thing I ask, before I can even think too much of it. The Oracle places her hand against her chest, bowing a little, her eyes full of sympathy.

"I apologize for the hurt this is causing you, but I am sure you are aware of how important it is that I stay safe."

"So you've placed a confusion spell on travelers as a test and then topped it off with a suppression spell for good measure?"

"Trinity." Rylan hisses a warning, but he should know better. I don't take my eyes off the Oracle as she studies me in return.

"You are a brilliant wolf, Trinity," she finally says, that smile back in place. "And you hold knowledge of the way of the witches."

"I lived among them for a time."

"Ah, yes. The Hawthornes. A powerful family, a powerful town."

"You know them?" For some reason, this surprises me. But why would it? They've done so much for the magical community in the last few years, I'm sure most of the world —and other realms—know about them.

"I know of them. They protect a great nexus of power, probably one of the greatest known to us. They have my gratitude. And respect."

Her words earn her a little bit of my respect. I'm not here to give that out to just anyone, but if she appreciates my friends for who they are, maybe I can give her a bit more benefit of the doubt.

"You told Rylan of how I am vital to saving the wolves," I say. "Can you tell me how I can help?"

She doesn't reply right away, turning to walk slowly between the flowers. We have no choice but to follow, waiting her out. Rylan walks a few feet behind me, keeping quiet. This is an interesting look on him. It's not one I think he's very comfortable with, but now is not the time to focus on that.

"Have you met any of these wolves?" the Oracles asks as she walks.

"Yes. We were attacked on the way here."

"What did you think of them?"

I'm not sure what kind of answer she expects here, but I don't see why I can't tell her what I told Zach.

"Their magic, their ability to shift, is missing." I can feel Rylan's eyes on me as I say so, and I'm surprised Zach didn't tell him of my suspicions. The Oracle however doesn't look even remotely surprised.

"It is what I was afraid of," she says, nodding her head slowly. I expect her to continue, but she doesn't. Her gaze simply turns to the tulips as she runs her hands over the delicate petals.

"How do I come into play?" I ask, hoping I won't have to beg her for every answer. Already, this is getting on my nerves. But I also know this is just the way things go, so I need to be patient. That's not exactly my best quality.

"Only you can answer that question, Trinity."

"What?"

That is absolutely not what I expected. Our whole trip here was so she could tell me how to help the wolves, how she prophesied for me to be the one to do so.

"I don't understand," Rylan says over my shoulder. It makes me feel better that I'm not the only one confused.

"You told him I was important."

"And you are. But only you can give yourself the answers you seek. I am here to merely guide you to them."

This is starting to sound more and more unnerving. I feel unprepared and unarmed. My wolf is buried so deep, she isn't of any help. I feel unbalanced by this, and even though I'm sure I can still fight physically, my mental strength is wavers. This has to be a trick, right?

"I can see that I have upset you." The Oracle finally turns back to us, that sympathetic look back on her face. "My words to the alpha were that you were necessary to the battle against what is happening to the shifters. But I do not know the precise journey you will take. Only the starting point."

Glancing back at Rylan, I see he's just as confused as I am.

But when his eyes meet mine, there's also a bit of confidence there. Confidence...in me. It's a glimpse of the Rylan of Before and it's enough for me to turn back to the Oracle and ask a question.

"What do I need to do?"

CHAPTER 14

The Oracle leads us farther into her garden in silence. When we reach a small opening between three tall trees, she motions for me to step inside. The area is about as big as a midsize sedan in diameter, and it dips slightly in the middle.

"Take a seat," she says, pointing to the middle of the clearing. I sit down, cross legged. "What you are about to do is go on a journey through the prophecies. This is something that has not been done in a long time, but it used to be the best way for a wolf to know his or her path."

"Like a vision quest?" I ask, and she smiles as she nods. I've heard of these. Dad used to tell me stories. Wolves would have to pass through sort of trials to win their position within the pack. It's an outdated practice and not something I've even thought of in years. They've only ever been stories.

"I thought vision quests were disbanded," Rylan comments, and the Oracle looks over at him.

"They are discouraged because there are no longer proper guides within the packs to make sure the quests are performed properly. Luckily for you, I am a professional."

The humor in her voice takes me by surprise. I definitely never thought of the Oracle as someone who jokes around. I really should stop putting any kind of expectations on this.

"Alpha, if you please."

She motions for Rylan to join me, and we both look at her as if she's crazy.

"He is part of your journey, Trinity. He will be your anchor."

None of that makes sense, but of course, Rylan doesn't even question her as he joins me in the middle of the small clearing.

"Take a seat, facing each other."

We do. And then, because we're so close, I can't seem to look away from him. The Oracle begins walking around us, muttering something, but all my attention is on the alpha in front of me. His eyes are the darkest I've ever seen, so deep blue they look almost black. He looks tired almost, and I'm sure I do as well. It's the pain of having our wolves nearly gone. It's draining us.

"Trinity, I need you to uncross your legs." It's takes me a second to realize the Oracle is looking at me.

"But—"

"Rylan, uncross yours, moving them to the side. Trinity, place yours cross his and scoot forward."

There's no way they can't hear my heartbeat speed up as I picture what that looks like. We will be chest to chest, our whole bodies pressed against each other, with me nearly straddling his hips.

"I don't—"

"This is non-negotiable," the Oracle says, stopping my protest. "Now, proceed."

Seeing no other choice, I pull my knees in as Rylan uncrosses his legs and places them on either side of me. Already, he is too close. Stretching out my own legs, I place them over his thighs, keeping my knees bent so as to not touch him more than necessary. Then I scoot forward.

Heat pools at the bottom of my stomach as every part of me brushes against him. Goosebumps explode across my skin as Rylan's arms wind around me, keeping me from moving back. I look up at him, finding him already looking at me. His jaw twitches just slightly, the only indication that this is affecting him at all.

"I don't think you need to—" I begin and am once again interrupted.

"Cross your legs behind Rylan, Trinity, and wrap your arms around his middle." When I look up at the Oracle as if she's lost her mind, she chuckles a little. "An anchor, Trinity. You need a physical hold on this world and that is what he is providing for you."

My breathing is quick. I try to find a way to control it before I completely lose it. I can feel Rylan in every part of me. I'm sure he can tell just how insane my heart is beating right now.

"Trinity." His voice is barely a whisper, and I look up at him. He's studying me with his typical Rylan intensity, but there's something else there. Just as I'm about to ask—or make a snarky remark—I feel a slight pressure at the base of my spine. My whole body tenses for a split second before a pleasant shiver travels up and over my back.

Rylan continues to move his thumb, ever so gently, up and down that one spot. I feel myself relax at the touch. I can't seem to look away from him. He seems to have the same problem.

"Good," the Oracle says. I have no idea exactly what she's talking about because all my attention is on that one simple touch. "When you are ready, close your eyes. I will guide you through it."

I think I might want to sit here like this for a very long time, so I force my eyes to close. Before I move even closer. My arms are around Rylan's chest, and it would be easy to simply lay my head there as well. But I don't. I need to keep my boundaries up.

"Trinity Whitewolf. You are traveling down a sacred path, a journey your ancestors took with an intention of guidance. It is your turn now. I will say a spell and you will travel into the unknown. Remember that everything you see has not happened yet. Most of it will not directly affect you. Rylan is there to pull you back, but he is also there for you to hold onto. Whatever you do, do not let go. Are you ready?"

"Yes."

I'm terrified and so many other things, but I am also determined. I hold onto that feeling.

"Then let's begin."

* * *

I DON'T HEAR whatever spell the Oracle utters. I don't feel anything but Rylan's thumb moving up and down my lower back.

Then, suddenly, I'm somewhere else.

I don't remember opening my eyes, but they are. I'm in the midst of a forest, much like the one I played in during my childhood, before my life changed. I can't feel my wolf at all. The empty feeling in my chest nearly takes me to my knees. But I can't succumb to such a display of emotion. I am here to find answers. The only thing I can do is move forward.

As I walk, I notice how everything seems to be almost muted in a way. The colors are dull. There are no birds or insects singing their typical songs. Even the air itself seems like it carries shadows within it. The trees stand tall but look like they're sick or dying. There's almost a film over the land, or as if I'm looking through dust-covered glasses. I move forward anyway. I need to figure this out. It would be nice if I knew what I was looking for, but of course, no such luck.

The stillness of the place creeps me out a little, if I'm going to be honest. The forest is always alive with sound. It's one of the things I love most about racing through the trees and bushes. This feels unreal and unnatural.

Something moves behind me. When I turn, there's barely a flash of white as the thing—whatever it is—disappears into the bushes. Without hesitation, I follow.

It moves fast, and I only catch glimpses of it as it weaves in and out of the trees. I know it's white because it's such a stark contrast to everything else here. There is a slight glow that surrounds it, but even with my supernatural eyesight, it's hard to follow. I'm not sure if that means I should be scared of it or not. For some reason, I don't feel any bad vibes coming off it or even off this place.

I know the Oracle said nothing here can hurt me, but that means nothing to me. I'd rather be prepared for any possibility. But I also know I can't keep chasing this thing all over this forest. Maybe there is a way to lure it out.

Moving forward, toward the last place I saw it, I walk slowly. When I'm on the other side of this row of trees, I see a pile of boulders. They create a hill of sorts. My inner wolf would love to lay up there under the full moon. Although, now that I think about it, the moon doesn't exist here. The sky is just dark.

The hill would give me an advantage, so I climb up there fast, giving my surroundings a quick study. Trees border around me as far as the eye can see. There are no openings, no clearings, no cliffs...it looks nothing like the forest I came from. I'm not sure why I thought it would. Maybe because this is my vision quest? It's the only explanation I have, but it doesn't matter, because that point is moot now. I'm nowhere near anything that looks even remotely familiar.

When a noise reaches me, I turn slowly. A wolf emerges from the woods, her eyes trained on me. Calling her a wolf seems irreverent, somehow. She's white, to the point where her fur glows an otherworldly type of glow. Her eyes are the most pure golden I have ever seen. She's huge, nearly the size of a horse. Even though everything around her is still, her fur moves as if it's dancing in the wind.

I can't take my eyes off her.

We stay like that for a while, her looking up at me as I stand at the top of the boulders. It puts us nearly eye to eye, which is incredible all in itself. I didn't think wolves her size existed anymore.

That's when I remember I'm in a vision, so they probably don't.

"I wouldn't be so sure of that."

The voice sounds directly in my head, like a pack link. It's gentle and tough at the same time. It instantly puts me at ease.

"So you are real?" I ask through the link as I take a step down the small hill.

"I am and I am not."

I nearly roll my eyes. "Someone else said that to me recently, and I find it annoying."

The moment the words are spoken, I realize how disrespectful they sound. But the wolf doesn't seem angry. In fact, she chuckles.

"You are who you are, Trinity. Don't ever minimize those parts of yourself."

There's a familiarity in the way she speaks to me, even in her voice. But I'm pretty sure I would've remembered meeting a nearly six-foot-tall shifter.

"So my sarcasm is who I am? Here I thought it was just a defense mechanism."

"Nothing about you is "just" anything. Your path is a lot more complicated than you could ever imagine."

"That sounds lovely."

The wolf chuckles again. I'm not sure why, but it makes me feel better that I am capable of making her laugh.

"What is it I'm supposed to do?" I ask, sobering up. The

wolf doesn't reply right away, walking a little bit to the side so I can come down from the boulders.

"You are about to go on a journey unlike any other and a choice will have to be made. What you choose will decide not only your own destiny, but that of those around you too."

"Does this have something to do with the rabid wolves?" My heart pounds now as my mind tries to catch up to the weight these words carry.

"Yes."

"Can you tell me what's wrong with the wolves?"

"I cannot. But you will learn of it soon enough, and it will be up to you to save them."

"How?" The moment I ask the question, everything around me begins to fade. "No, I'm not done. How do I help them?"

"By being true to yourself. If you learn one truth from me it is that you are more capable than you think and stronger than you believe. No one can take your power away from you. You can only give it away. Don't give it away. Don't let anyone stand in your way. Find your magic and use it."

With that last word, the wolf fades into the forest and then the forest fades into nothingness. I call out, but my voice simply echoes all around. My mind is completely disoriented. I can't seem to find which way is up or down. I drop to my knees as I stumble. Everything seems to be slipping through my fingers. I can't get a grip on what's real and what's not.

A voice calls my name—a voice I know. I turn toward it, and when I do, I feel a slight pressure at the base of my back. Then it all comes rushing in.

Rylan. The Oracle. The vision quest.

The slight pressure, I know for a fact it's Rylan. I focus on the feel of his touch. Suddenly, I'm opening my eyes and he's right in front of me.

"Trinity."

"I'm okay, I'm okay." I breath heavily, sweat dripping down my temples. My hands sting, and I realize I've been gripping Rylan's shirt tightly. Flexing my fingers, I let go. Then scoot back as much as our position allows me to do.

"What did you see?" the alpha asks, all of his attention on me. Images and bits of conversation race through my mind, but I can't hold onto any of it long enough to remember. They're slipping away before I could even grab on.

"Why can't I remember?" I ask, turning to the Oracle, who's been standing quietly to the side.

"You will. Your mind is reconfiguring itself to reality once more. You will be able to recall what happened in a few hours at the most."

I nod, before I slowly—very slowly—push away from Rylan and untangle my legs from around him. He doesn't hold onto me, giving me my space, as he gets to his feet. I follow suit a little more slowly, still reeling from that strange experience.

Somehow though, I don't think I got all the answers I could've. That makes me concerned.

CHAPTER 15

*T*he Oracle leads us back the way we came, offering us a glass of water each. I drink mine like I've been thirsty for days, still having a hard time organizing my thoughts. This time, I let Rylan do the thanking.

"You are welcome to return at any time," the Oracle says to me.

"You don't want to know what my vision showed me?" I ask. I would have thought the Oracle would want more answers regarding her own visions about me.

"It is not my place to know or the vision would have revealed itself to me. Now, I have performed my duty, and it is time for you to go."

I'm not going to lie, it seems like the Oracle is kicking us out. Honestly, I'm okay with it though, because the sooner we leave, the sooner I can feel my wolf again. But I'm not about to walk away so easily.

"What was the point of this if I can't even remember it?"

"This place," she waves a hand around the beautiful garden, "it's a doorway of sorts. It opens up magics deep inside of you. Those you may not even know you carry. You know about magic, don't you?" I know exactly what she means by that question.

"You mean the witches?"

The Oracle nods.

"What you carry with you from your time with them, use it."

I can feel Rylan's dislike immediately even without having to look at him. Shifters aren't known to trust witches.

"She will guide you," the Oracle turns to Rylan, "Trust her."

Cryptic, but I can't disagree with that one. He should listen to me more. Then, it's like she's done with us. Even if I wanted to ask more questions, she seems to have completely dismissed us.

We walk out the way we came in. When I step through, the tree shimmers behind me until they are solid bark again. Turning, I see Rylan watching me. I shake my head.

"I don't want to talk about it."

"You have to tell me *something*."

"I don't know anything. All I have are these strong emotions, mostly fear and confusion. That doesn't exactly help us, does it?"

"You're saying this was a waste of time?"

"I don't know what I'm saying," I nearly yell, frustration running through my veins. "Just get me back to my wolf and we'll go from there."

Rylan doesn't move right away, that intense look back in

his eyes. But I have no answers for him, and it's more frustrating than I'd like to admit.

"Think, Trinity. There has to be something."

Rolling my shoulders back, I begin to walk, not waiting to see if Rylan follows. I'm angry at the Oracle, at the useless way she delivered information, at how there's almost no information. How could she have given Rylan such a sure guidance on the importance of me being back and then give me nothing on what that actually means?

"Trinity."

"Stop, just stop it." I twirl around, and he's right behind me. I nearly stumble into him. I see his hands reach for me as I take step back. "You pushing isn't going to reset my brain any faster. You'll just have to wait and see."

"And trust that you're not holding anything back?"

The words are spoken quietly, but they hold so much weight in them I'm nearly overcome. This is what it's all about—trust. He doesn't trust me.

"If you have such terrible faith in me, then you should've left me out of it," I reply, placing my hands on my hips as I stare him down.

"Well excuse me if I don't put much faith in someone who is known to break my trust."

The anger I carry with me consistently rises up to the surface at his words. They're like cuts slicing open scabbed over wounds, making them bleed all over. The history between us assaults me from every side. I feel every emotion I felt as a youngling.

"You didn't exactly end up completing your part of the bargain either," I snap.

"No, you will not turn this around on me. You knew what you were doing."

"I was a pup!" I yell, fury blurring my vision. "My parents were missing too, what was I supposed to do?"

"You were supposed to trust me!" he snaps, anger burning hotter than the sun in his eyes. "I was going to—I would've taken care of you."

"But no," he says before I can speak up. "You had to be stubborn. Even back then, you had to take things into your own hands. You broke sacred pack law."

"You don't think I know that? You don't think I regret sharing our village's location with the—"

"An outsider, Trinity!" There's that anger again. "You let a stranger into our midst and because of that my *father* is dead!"

His words are like a slap, even though I'm ready for the accusations. Well, maybe not quite this one. His dad? I'm not sure what he means by that, but if that's what he thinks—I can't let myself fall apart right now. He's hurt and angry and he won't listen to reason. Not right now. Taking a deep breath, I force myself to process.

We both made mistakes, but I will never forgive myself for sharing the White Wolf village location with an outsider. Even though it was unintentional. I've had to carry that with me for years. But Rylan isn't as innocent in all this as he pretends to be.

We're both breathing heavily, face to face, the forest more alive around us than ever. It feels like there is almost no distance between us at all, and yet, we're too far apart. My head spins, my body is on fire.

I can't tell if I'm responding to him, to my memories, or to the desires I buried away long ago.

One thing I know about us is that neither one will be the first to yield. That is not how we are made. We'll stand here in this silent battle of wills for an eternity. That is why I'm the one to break the eye contact first, spinning away, and stomping into the woods.

We're never going to see eye to eye. We just need to get through this and then we'll never have to spend this much time in each other's company ever again.

* * *

It takes almost no time to get back to where we can finally...finally shift. The moment I feel my wolf inside me, I don't hesitate. My limbs move and then I'm running as a wolf, and everything is right in the world once more. It may seem strange to talk about her as another being, but she is me, and I am her, and yet we're different. And right now, we're two pieces that have finally come together again.

Rylan races beside me. I don't have to ask to know how he's feeling. There's a sense of joy about him—the same one I'm experiencing—and for the one moment, I actually feel like part of his pack.

Since there are no confusion spells on us, we make progress in a straight line. In half a day, we're on the outskirts of town, and Rylan finally slows down. He shifts back, turning to face me. I follow suit, confused.

"What is it?"

"I want to talk about what you saw. Before we join the others."

"There's nothing more to say." I shrug because it's true. I have no answers for him or for myself. Technically, I know the trip wasn't a waste. I understand I've been given a path to follow. But I have nothing figured out, no memories have returned while we were running, so it's pointless to rehash things.

Also, I don't want to think about his arms around me. Or the way he keeps pulling me back from the darkness. Or the argument we had afterward.

"Trinity."

"Don't pull that alpha voice with me, Rylan. You know it doesn't work."

He growls in response, taking a step toward me.

"We're going to do this every time?"

"Absolutely," I reply, grinning. He blinks, as if blinded, and I realize it might be the first time I've actually smiled at him since I've come back. He seems stunned for a moment before he shakes it off.

We're so all over the place, we're volatile together.

"Look, it was probably not the right time to have that conversation—"

"Don't you dare apologize," I say, narrowing my gaze on him. "I haven't remembered anything. I know I should by now, but I haven't. I can't tell if it's because I'm tired or hungry or what. But there's nothing. *Nothing.*"

It makes me feel pretty useless, if I'm going to be honest with myself. But I'm not about to give into the frustration.

Rylan's expression changes, but I truly can't tell what he's thinking. I wonder if he's going to yell at me again. I'm ready for it, but then a noise catches my attention. Rylan and I turn just in time to watch Zach and Ezra step into the woods.

"I take it, it didn't go well," Zach says, his eyes shifting between Rylan and me.

"It went fine," I snap, pushing past the two guys and walking towards the town. "I need a change of clothes. And a shower."

Without waiting to see if anyone will follow, I make my way to the main street. From what I remember, there's a motel situated on the corner. And a store right next to it.

What I need is a shower, a new dress, and some time away from Rylan. Before I completely explode.

CHAPTER 16

When I step into the store, I realize I have no money. Back in Hawthorne, the alpha had a deal with the town, a sort of a running tab. I didn't have to worry about stuff like money. But I can't exactly get a new change of clothes or a hotel room with a bathtub with just smiles.

Dejected, I turn to go back out when Ezra steps inside the store behind me. His eyes meet mine. He pats his pocket, nodding his head in the direction of the clothes at the back of the store. I grin up at him. He blinks, much like Rylan did, as if stunned. He looks slightly confused by his own response, and I decide to help the poor guy out. With my signature sarcasm.

"So did you draw the short straw?" I ask, turning toward a rack of t-shirts. Ezra makes a noise much like a chuckle would sound, if he actually ever laughed, before I hear his grumpy voice.

"I volunteered."

"Ah, I see. Did you need to make up some community hours or something?" I'm looking through clothes, but I glance up in time to see Ezra trying to suppress a smile.

"Don't make me regret this," he says instead.

"I'm sure you already do," I say over my shoulder and move farther into the store.

They don't have many options, so I'll probably have to settle on shorts and a tank, but I'm not done looking yet. The distance away from Rylan is giving my mind some rest. The intensity that is constantly present between us can be overwhelming at times. Not that I'd admit that to anyone. In fact, I will deny it if asked.

It's frustrating that I can't remember what happened on my vision quest, but it's even more frustrating when I have an alpha staring me down, waiting for answers.

The only reason he agreed we'd go see the Oracle is because he too needed to understand why I had to return. Now it feels like we've taken a few steps backward. Again.

Shaking my head, I try to push away the conversation that's playing on repeat in my mind. The anger I heard in Rylan's voice when he accused me of his father's death. I've heard it before, and it hurt me just as much this time as it did all those years ago.

I made a mistake, but I know for a fact it wasn't my fault the alpha died. But explaining that to Rylan would be like talking to a brick wall. He didn't want to hear me then. He's not going to hear me now.

All I can really do is keep my head down, try and remember what happened during the vision quest, and use that to help the wolves. That's it. Everything else is irrelevant.

"You know, he changed." Ezra's voice breaks through my thoughts and I turn to glance at him.

"What do you mean?" I ask, when he doesn't continue. I think he's surprised he spoke up at all. He looks away, searching for something over my shoulder, before his deep brown eyes focus on me once more.

"After you—left. He changed. His whole identity became being an alpha, something he wasn't ready to be yet. He stopped laughing. He stopped talking. He became a completely different man. And wolf."

I hold my breath as he speaks, processing his words with my mind. Even though it's my heart that wants to get involved.

"Why are you telling me this?" I finally ask.

Ezra doesn't answer right away. "I think both of you carry a lot of heavy weight. But maybe if you understand nothing is that black and white—"

"If you're trying to make excuses for him—"

"I'm not. I'm simply telling you how things were. You can make your own conclusions from the information given."

He turns away then, and I go back to looking through the racks as his words ring through my mind. I don't want them to change anything, but I can't help wondering. He was always a tough wolf, but there was softness about him when he was around me. I still see glimpses of it in him. But I can also see the changes.

It's the same changes I've went through. Life is a hell of a thing to happen to a person, and we all process it in our own way.

I'm about to grab a pair of shorts when I see it. A strip of red peeks out from between the clothes hanging on the rack across from me. It's one of those circular ones, where hangers are pushed together as tightly as they will go, so it's easy to miss things unless you go through each item.

I'm across the room in a second, tugging the material out. I know I'm grinning even before I fully pull it out.

"You've got to to be kidding me." I turn toward Ezra's surprised words, holding the dress against me.

"It's meant to be!" I bounce on the balls of my feet, unable to contain my excitement. There's a dressing room at the back, and I don't even bother grabbing other pieces of clothes as I head there.

Once inside, I pull my own dress over my head with one yank. The poor thing has been through a lot and I thank it for its service. The dress I hold in my hands now looks like it was made just for me.

With only spaghetti straps, it has a sweetheart neckline and a small cutout detail at the front, right over my stomach. I pull it over my head, and it settles against my curves as if it is meant to be there. The hem is rounded with an extra layer underneath. It's one of those skater dresses, and the color is of peonies, and I'm absolutely obsessed. It comes down mid-thigh, longer than the dress I've been wearing. But only because Rylan took a chuck of it, while binding my wound.

Just that small thought brings back the sensation of his teeth grazing my thigh, and then I'm in the small meadow, his arms holding me close as I take a trip into the vision quest.

My body heats up at the thought, and I force the reaction away. They're nothing but my hormones reacting to a gorgeous man and wolf. I have to keep it in check.

I also have to buy this dress.

Changing out of it quickly, I step out and grab some underwear as well before heading to the counter. I'm not sure how these wolves live, but I need my luxuries. Which means next order of business is a bath.

* * *

WHEN WE ARRIVE at the hotel, Rylan and Zach have a room ready. And by that, I mean just the one room.

"You expect me to stay here with the lot of you?" I ask as Ezra and I walk in. My eyes scan the small surroundings. There's one bed in the middle of the room, one nightstand, and a table with a television on it. That's it. I turn just as the door to my left opens, and a half-naked Rylan steps out into the room. My mind shuts down completely at the sight of his glistening chest. When I remember to tear my gaze away, he's already watching me with a knowing smirk.

I roll my eyes, stepping back, but the tiny hallway leaves no room for Rylan. He brushes against me as he steps into the room. That's when I realize Zach looks freshly showered as well and dressed in clean jeans and a t-shirt. The guys must've bought clothes while Ezra and I were gone.

My skin still buzzes from Rylan's proximity and I have a

feeling the shifters can tell. I need to find my footing again. Snarky remarks for the win.

"You better not have used all the hot water," I call out. I catch a glimpse Rylan's narrowed eyes as I step into the bathroom and shut the door. With that small barrier between us, I try to calm my racing heart.

If I don't learn how to control my weird reactions to Rylan, I will not survive.

My mind goes over everything we have done so far. I know what our next move is. We need to head back to the pack. He's already been away too long, and if we're going to get anywhere with protecting them, we need to be there. In the meantime, I need to figure out what in the world I'm supposed to do.

Stripping out of my clothes quickly and taking the makeshift bandage off my wrist, I get into the shower. The scratches on the wound have healed over, but I can still feel them there. Maybe it's just the idea of the tattoo from my dream that I notice. It's almost as if it's under the surface, somehow. I know it's a tattoo, but I still can't grasp the full image. My mind seems to be playing with me on all kinds of levels right now.

I let water run over my skin, washing away the days spent traveling. I love being in nature, but that doesn't mean I don't like my human perks, like feeling of hot water trailing down my skin. It soothes and nourishes. I needed this.

I try not to think about the guys on the other side of the door, but I can't help it. They're probably discussing everything that's happened through the pack link because I can't hear anyone saying anything. With my supernatural hearing,

I should be able to pick up their conversation, even over running water. But I guess they're back to keeping their secrets.

It's not like I'm not keeping secrets. Mine are just buried somewhere in my head where I can't access them, so it doesn't count. My mind latches onto what happened in those woods and then my body reacts accordingly. All my skin is aflame as I think about Rylan's arms around me.

Pushing those thoughts away is harder than I'd like to admit, but I know the guys will be able to pick up my emotions. Even through the door. At least Rylan will, and I don't need to give him any more ammunition against me.

Even though I'm not excited about returning to the home and the pack that abandoned me, a part of me is excited to run through those woods again. There is something particularly special about a wolf and their connection to their home. We're connected to it in a way that's unique to us. While Hawthorne was home for six years, I was never able to fully connect to the forest there. It was a constant reminder that I didn't really belong there.

My wolf is right beneath my skin, almost nudging the memories my way. But when I start to think about the forest, the images in my mind change.

Slowly at first and then with lighting speed. Image after image of a forest filled with…shadow and gloom bombard me. My head feels like it's about to split in two. I grab it with my hands, trying to keep it from exploding. The breath in my lungs is constraining, and then I can't seem to breathe at all. Pain shakes my body, and I drop to my knees, curling into myself, just as a loud bang sounds around me. I can't tell if it's coming from inside of me or not. One image after the other shoots pain straight into my brain.

The panic I feel squeezes the air out of my lungs, and I'm shaking all over. I don't know which way is up or down, and it feels like I'm drowning. Right where I lay. I can't seem to control my body as it reacts in an unusual way. I can't think, all I do is feel, and it's too much.

Suddenly, the water is turned off and someone is beside me in the shower. A towel is placed over my shoulders and then I'm being picked up and gently held against a strong chest. I can feel arms around me as I stay curled into myself and against the warmth. It's an automatic response. I cling to the safety I feel surround me.

Just as quickly as the images came, they recede. My body finds balance as the arms hold me closer. When I am able to lift my head, I realize I'm on Rylan's lap, cradled against him, right there in the shower. It takes me even longer to realize I'm naked, but then I feel the towel against my skin and am a bit confused and grateful. That was definitely for my benefit. Shifters have no care for modesty. And the fact that there's only a small piece of cloth separating our bodies makes me blush. So, of course, I go on the offensive.

"What are you doing?" I ask, pushing away from Rylan. There's a fierce protectiveness in his gaze when he meets my eye. It's not something I have ever seen in him. Slightly similar to how we were as kids, but with a whole new level of intensity added to it. I can't quite explain what I see or feel. It makes my whole body come alive, and I push against him harder. This time, he lets go.

He shifts his body to the side so I can stand, pushing me

out of the tub at the same time. I grab the towel, wrapping it tightly against me as he steps out into the tiny bathroom beside me.

"I was trying to keep you from clawing your eyes out," Rylan says. It takes me a moment to remember I asked him a question.

"What?"

"Last time you sent out such powerful emotional distress, you clawed your wrist raw. Didn't want a repeat performance."

I stare up at him, meeting his eyes in the mirror. He's right behind my left shoulder, and we're standing side by side because it's the only way we fit in the bathroom. He takes up most of the space. I don't think I've ever realized how small I look beside him.

"You going to tell me about it?" he asks, his eyes still on me in the mirror.

"It was one image. Over and over. A forest, maybe dying, maybe dead. But gloomy and...forgotten...no, almost forgotten." I'm not sure what that distinction means, but I feel like I have to make it.

"Do you think it was a memory of your quest?"

I wish he would move. I wish we could have this conversation somewhere other than a cramped bathroom where the only armor I have is a flimsy towel.

"It's the only explanation. The Oracle didn't mention it would be like this."

"No, she did not." That fierce protectiveness is back in his gaze. He stares at me for a moment longer before he steps behind me and out on the other side, leaving the imprint of his body heat against my already heated skin.

I go to close the door, but I see that it's off its hinges. With a gulp, I realize I have no other option. Dropping the towel, I try to catch my breath as I get dressed.

CHAPTER 17

$\mathcal{W}$e leave the tiny room behind after finishing off the food Zach picked up while I was in the shower. There's not much for us to do in town, and everyone—except me—is itching to get back to the pack. I'm not trying to be difficult about it. I just have a lot of conflicting feelings on the matter.

I'm also having conflicting thoughts on what in the world is going on with Rylan. I can tell he still hates me. The argument we had in the woods sits heavy upon my heart. Yet, this is the second time he's come to my rescue—in a way. And shown a response to me I don't understand. Now, he's ignoring me, like I'm the bane of his existence. Truly, I hope I am. He deserves a little torture in his life.

He didn't comment on my dress, but I saw the way his eyes raked over me. A little torture in a red dress. That's me.

The only explanation I can come up with is that it's his

alpha-ness. He can't help it. He maybe a tough boss, but he takes care of his own. And technically, I am one of his now.

I can honestly say I don't know how I feel about that statement. I mostly hate it, but also...not? This all is becoming way too complicated for me.

We shift the moment we step into the woods, and Rylan opens up the pack link to me.

"We'll travel south until sundown. That should take us to the creek. We'll rest there before traveling the rest of the way in the morning."

Just like that, the link shuts off again. Rylan takes off. Zach waits beside me as Ezra follows Rylan. I give him a look that says I know it's his turn to be my watch wolf. They're taking this position pretty seriously. If I wasn't so annoyed, I'd feel touched. Or something. Mostly I'm just annoyed.

At Rylan.

This whole thing he's doing with the pack link is intentional. I refuse to call him out on it because I know that's exactly what he wants. He's playing his little games, while I play mine. I intend to win—with every fiber of my being.

But running through the woods again does help clear my mind. If only a little bit. The images I saw in my near panic state gave me no answers, but they did raise questions. Why wouldn't the Oracle mention this kind of mental assault? Why didn't she prepare me for the possibility?

I'm still way more confused about her and the whole quest than ever before. It's more than frustrating to have my mind messed with and then having no idea how or even why. What did the Oracle gain from us coming to see her? There had to be something, right?

The only saving grace I have is that Rylan was there the whole time. I will never admit this out loud, but him serving as my anchor not only helped pull me out of my...whatever that was. It also helps me now, knowing that I wasn't left at the mercy of the Oracle.

Just as I think that, another thought slams into me. What if they were in on it? What if both Rylan and the Oracle manipulated me?

But no. That doesn't taste true. If there was even an ounce of me that believed that Rylan was in on it, I wouldn't feel so strongly about his innocence on this particular matter. If there is one thing Rylan has always been it's protective of his pack. He already proved that he would protect me. If I trust nothing else about him, then I do at least trust that.

It still leaves me in a weird position though.

And pretty helpless if I'm being honest.

The sun begins to set before I realize it's happening. We've been traveling for a few hours, keeping a steady pace. I don't recognize these woods just yet, but I can tell Zach and Ezra do. They've stayed pretty close to me through the whole day, and I can feel excitement coming off them now. We must be closer than I realized.

When the sound of water reaches my ears, I perk up. Traveling at this speed sure makes me thirsty. We burst through the trees in another few minutes and then the most beautiful sight greets me. A whole creek full of fresh, clean water flows ahead of us. I race to it before I know what I'm doing. At the last moment, I stop.

"*It's safe to drink.*" Rylan's voice sounds in my mind,

jarring me for a second. I didn't think he'd opened the link up again. But I'm not going to comment. I start drinking instead. The others follow suit.

When we've had our fill, the boys shift and spread out to search for firewood.

"We're camping here?" I ask.

"Right over there," Rylan replies, pointing to the right. I see a wall of trees and a cleared out area, like someone has camped here before. The way the guys seem perfectly at home, I'm sure that's true.

In no time at all, we have a fire burning and some fowls of the air cooking. This all feels a lot more homey than I would like to admit out loud.

WE EAT our fill and then settle in for the night. The guys are talking about some river they found on a survey trip once, but I'm not listening. My mind keeps going over the images that came to me in the shower.

Getting to my feet, I proceed to pace, hoping to work off some of the nervous energy that creeps over my body. The new dress I'm wearing is light on my skin. I run my hands over it a little to feel the fabric.

"You look ridiculous in that dress."

The words are barely audible, but I hear them. Spinning around, I pin Rylan with a look. He doesn't see it since he keeps his eyes on the fire.

"You know I look fabulous," I reply with a grin, as I run my hand over the material again. He started this with his comment. He should know I'm not just going to let it pass. When his eyes snag on mine, I can see he didn't miss the way I moved my hands over my curves.

"You can't fight in that."

Ezra and Zach grow completely quiet, now watching our exchange. I narrow my eyes at Rylan before I reply.

"Are you telling me what I can and cannot do again? What handbook tells you that girls can't fight while wearing dresses?"

"I don't need a handbook," Rylan snaps. "I have eyes."

"Oh I know you do. I've seen them wander all over this dress you hate *so* much."

Rylan's head jerks up at that, his eyes piercing. I'm pretty sure he's pinned me to the spot. The turbulence of emotions inside me makes my head spin. It's Zach's muffled chuckle that helps me keep my wits about me, I turn to him with a grin.

"Fabulous and hilarious," I comment. "The whole package."

Then I do something that for sure infuriates Rylan. I take the corners of my skirt into my hands and curtsey, glancing at him from under my eyelashes. He was tending to the fire, and now he's gripping the stick too hard. It looks like it's about to...snap.

And there it goes.

My body reacts to that look again, his precise Rylan look. I can't allow that.

"I bet you I could take both Zach and Ezra in this dress and not even break a sweat." At my challenge, the boys sit up. No one challenges a wolf unless ready to follow through.

Honestly, I could use a little bit of practice. It's been way too long.

"Come on," I say, raising an eyebrow. "Don't tell me you're scared."

The wolves growl at me as one, and I try not to smile. They're so easy to read. I need one last little push, and that's all it'll take.

"Come on, boys. I'm sure *you* could use the practice."

There it is. That has the desired effect. They take one look at Rylan. When he doesn't stop them, they come at me. Large and strong, they're quick on their feet. But I didn't spend so much of my childhood learning to fight as a human to be outsmarted now.

Both Zach and Ezra are much taller than me, but I can use that to my advantage. They step around me, on each side. They probably aren't expecting much. That is why I'm the one who attacks first.

Quick on my feet, I round kick Ezra until he stumbles at least seven feet back. Zach has a moment of hesitation from the surprise, but then he's moving on me. I drop low as he swings, bringing my fist up into his stomach. He stumbles back from the blow, and I jump to my feet to kick him back. Ezra is there next, his arms winding around me as he pins me to his chest. Instead of struggling, I go limp. His grip slips for a split second, but in that time, I find my footing. Using his own body against him, I flip him over my back. Both Zach and Ezra are in front of me now. I have to push the hair out of my face. It dried wild while we ran, but I don't care. I'm having fun.

The guys move forward as one, throwing punches I block

easily. I shift my body from one side to the other as I block and deliver my own punches. It's a dance of sorts, and I don't hesitate to be the one leading. When my fist slams into Zach's face, I follow it up with a knee to the stomach. As Ezra swings at me, I twist, using Zach as a shield before I toss him at Ezra. My supernatural strength, coupled with years of practice, make that little toss painful enough to knock the wind out of their lungs.

I straighten, pushing my hair over one shoulder. Then I glance over at Rylan. He watches the whole exchange with an intensity I don't want to name. Straightening my dress, I do another small curtsey. Rylan's eyes flash.

"How's that for a girl in a dress?"

Rylan doesn't reply but continues to watch me. I can't hold his gaze as long as I would like to. Goosebumps start at the base of my spine. I tear my eyes away to look at the other two. They're getting off the ground now, and I reach a hand down to them.

"No hard feelings?"

I think Ezra is going to hold a grudge, but Zach seems excited.

"Where did you learn how to fight like that?" he asks, accepting my hand as I pull him up.

"Jay. He's one of the wolves in Jefferson's pack. He taught me hand-to-hand combat from the beginning. I can take care of myself in any form."

"It's impressive. We haven't trained like that in years. Not since—" He doesn't say it, but we all know. Not since I left. Because that was something Rylan's dad did for the pack, teach them how to be human.

"Well, I'd be happy to show you a few pointers," I say, and we leave it at that. Ezra sits back down by the fire. I can see his ego is bruised, but he's impressed. Zach, on the other hand, doesn't seem fazed at all. So, I take a seat next to him, ignoring the Alpha, and chat about different styles of fighting.

CHAPTER 18

*T*hat night I almost expect dreams or memories, but there's nothing. It's like my mind has completely shut down. Not that I'm not grateful. I'm exhausted. It feels like I've been going nonstop for months, instead of days.

However, a quiet mind also makes it difficult to sleep. I'm not sure how I'm supposed to deal with that either. I decide to sleep in my human form, stretching out beside the fire. When I turn to the side, I scan the forest and the creek. I can make out the shape of Rylan in his wolf form, standing near the water.

There's a moment where I get an overwhelming urge to go to him, but I squish it down. We're not friends, we're not —anything really. I have no right to know his thoughts or emotions.

Closing my eyes, I take a few deep breaths, trying to calm my spirit. Everything seems to be moving too fast and yet not fast enough. Less than two weeks ago, I thought my life would go a very specific way. And here I am, moving in a completely different direction.

Concentrating on my breathing, I calm my mind and my body, willing it to rest. I have no idea what to expect tomorrow, how the pack will receive me, and that's causing anxiety. For me and my wolf.

I can feel her worry and her longing for acceptance. We were not meant to be lone wolves. We need a home, a pack, and tomorrow, I get to see if that's a possibility for me. Or if I'm always going to be an outsider.

When I finally do drift off to sleep, I don't even realize it.

This dream doesn't feel anything like the ones I've been experiencing for the past few weeks. It's more of a gentle change in the air, instead of an abrupt fall. I find myself in the woods once more. It's true what they say I guess, a wolf goes where it is the most comfortable. My dreams are always in the woods because I don't feel at home anywhere else.

The forest around me is different from the others I've been in. The colors are bright. The scents of the fresh flowers reach out to me, even though I don't see any. The only difference between this and reality is that I don't hear any animals or insects. I've noticed that before, I think. I can't quite remember.

The feeling of being watched slams into me. I can't tell if it's me or the wolf who feels it first, but I twist around, my eyes zeroing in on the movement to my right. Before I can think too much, or react in anyway, the beast bursts out of the greenery, leaping straight at me.

It's a wolf, about four feet tall, bigger than I am in my

wolf form. I scream as the wolf lands on top of me, pinning my body underneath him. Saliva drips from his open mouth. The smell of rotten flesh slaps me in the face. I try to wiggle free, to use some of my fighting skills, but it's like I'm completely helpless.

I can't move. I can't force my limbs to listen to my commands.

This beast is going to tear me apart, and there is nothing I can do about it.

Tears pool in my eyes as I refuse to accept my demise. This is not how I'm going out. I refuse to be taken by surprise by some deformed beast and not fight. He leans down, opening his mouth more, as if he's getting ready to take a chunk out of my flesh. That's when I hear my name.

It's soft, barely a whisper in the wind, but I realize this isn't real. This is a dream.

The moment I remember that, the wolf disappears. Then I am back in the real forest, opening my eyes. The first thing I see is Rylan, still by the river, but his full attention is on me. I can feel his alpha powers reaching out toward me, as if he knew I needed him. My heart beats a mile a second. I force myself up to my elbows, if only to have something to do.

Looking back to Rylan, I see that he hasn't moved. He also hasn't taken his eyes off me.

"I'm okay," I whisper, but I know he can hear me. He holds my gaze another moment before he turns back around.

I start my breathing exercises, pushing air into my lungs. These dreams are getting too strange for my liking. And I'm getting tired of Rylan coming to my rescue. Even though I'm grateful he can.

* * *

Rylan doesn't mention my weird middle-of-the-night wake up. By the time morning comes, he's back to ignoring me entirely. That is honestly fine, because I am stressing out. We have barely half a day journey left, and then I'll be—well, not home. But the closest place I can call that.

My wolf is so excited. She can't wait to run free through the forest, to feel the dirt of her childhood under her paws. It's the human side of me that's overthinking everything. I haven't been this unsure of myself in six years.

It doesn't take us long to reach the familiar hill, the one that overlooks the village below. I asked my dad once why give the enemy such an advantage, of having a way to sneak up on us from above. He simply replied that it made it easier to hide below. I never did ask him what he meant by that.

With my mind lost in memories, I don't even realize we have arrived.

Rylan howls as he stops on the hill overlooking the village. I don't see it yet, but I can feel that it's there. The pack answers back, Zach and Ezra joining. My heart wants to jump out of my chest. My wolf nearly leaps from the feel of the forest around her. Rylan howls again and then there's a moment of silence and I know he's speaking to the pack through the link.

Then, he turns to look at me, opening that link to me.

"Trinity."

Just my name. Nothing else. But I feel that sound in every cell in my body. My chest hurts, my head spins, and then I take a step forward.

Moving slowly, I make my way toward Rylan to stand beside him on the hill. He's presenting me to the pack, much like Jefferson did when he brought me in. And just like Rylan did when he cast me out.

The overwhelming tirade of emotions threaten to drown me. I want to say I'm stronger than this, that I can hold my head up high and not be affected by the stares of the pack that was supposed to protect me and didn't. When I stop beside Rylan, my eyes are still on him. I can tell he's going through his own slew of emotions. I can't even begin to name them as they race through his eyes. He knows it's his duty as the alpha to welcome me back, that it's his job to set the example and make the rest of them follow. But I can also see the struggle within him. The hurt of our past, mingled with the reality of our future. He's just as unbalanced as I am. That fact gives me the confidence I need to tear my gaze away and look out over the village.

It looks exactly how I remember it. Small houses are built between tall trees. They are hidden from the world, apart but also enough a part of it to have modern conveniences. Lights hang overhead, and I can hear running water in the pipes below.

The pack looks up at me as I study them in return. There are so many faces, all matured by the years I've been gone. Yet, they're familiar enough to bring a pang of hurt and sadness to my heart. And yes, even a bit of happiness. I feel it, even though I don't want to. Even though they don't deserve it from me. Not the longing, not the forgiveness. They failed me just like Rylan did. But I also know I played a part in that. I think I've finally accepted my role.

I raise my chin a little higher, my fur moving in the gentle breeze. There's silence as I get reacquainted with the pack and the forest around it.

Then, only then, does Rylan do the one thing he hasn't done since I met him. He opens up the pack link to the whole pack, including me, all at once.

"Trinity Whitewolf. Welcome back."

There's a moment of stillness as the words wash over every single wolf in the pack. I feel the pack's magic, that unique shifter spark, wash over me. And then, something completely unexpected happens.

My wolf goes absolutely crazy. I try to keep still, but she needs to be heard. Even though I know it's not my place, even though I know I'm not supposed to, I can't control it. I lift my head, and I howl straight into the sky.

There isn't a moment of hesitation as the rest of the pack repeats my cry. Everything around me begins to glow. I can't shut my eyes against the light, but I also can't seem to stop it surrounding me. The wolves continue to howl. So do I. And then I'm in the midst of light and sound and sensations like I've never experienced before.

I can feel each and every wolf. I can hear their thoughts, read their emotions. They're just as surprised—panicked almost—and then, the light dissipates.

I'm out of breath, my body buzzing from whatever magic is still working its way through me. I glance at Rylan and the absolute shock I find there nearly brings me to the ground. He can't stop staring at me, but it's different. It's not like I'm used to him looking at me at all. We continue to watch each other, and I can tell he's demanding answers with his eyes, but I have nothing to give him.

"*Alpha?*"

Rylan and I swivel our heads in unison toward Zach, who's watching us very carefully. His eyes bounce between the two of us. When I meet his eyes, he looks shocked and in awe and confused all at the same time.

"*I heard you,*" I say, but it shouldn't have been possible. Not when he specifically reached out to his alpha. Zach starts to reply, but Rylan's growl stops him. I move my attention back to him.

"*You—how is this—I don't understand.*" Only broken pieces of his words reach out to me, as if he's trying to shut off the link, but it's not working. And that's when I realize why it's not.

Because I'm alpha.

CHAPTER 19

To say the pack is in chaos would be an understatement. Rylan shifts as soon as we make it down to the village, and I follow suit, not knowing what else to do. He grabs me by the upper arm, yanking me into a house without ceremony. Every part of me wants to rebel against such rough handling, but I keep control. He's angry, his alpha is angry, and I'm simply overwhelmed and confused.

"What did you do?" He growls, getting right in my face. Okay, just like that, the confusion is gone, replaced by my own anger.

"Me? What did you do?" I throw back at him. He blinks at me, as if he's surprised I talk back, but he should be used to it by now. I've done it from the very beginning.

"What could I have done?" Rylan asks, pointing a finger at me. "You've got all those witch friends. Did you cook something up with them? Did you come here to destroy my pack?"

He's barely holding it together. His body shakes with rage. Zach and Ezra are behind him, in the doorway. I have no doubt the whole pack can hear us screaming at each other. Well, fine. If he wants to play that card, let him.

"You want to start throwing blame around again? I know how good you are at that," I snap, not bothering to lower my voice or step back. He doesn't miss what I'm doing, his eyes flash in awareness.

"I would be very careful here, princess. You don't want to go head to head with me."

The natural way he uses the nickname unbalances me for a moment. I blink against the memories and the feelings I've tried so hard to bury. I don't even know if he even remembers he called me that when we were young. Either way, I'm not about to let one word deter me.

"I think you *need* someone to go head to head with you. Teach you a lesson."

He growls again, getting right into my face. Even though I have to look up at him, I hold my ground.

"As if you could do anything but run away." He nearly spits the words at me, and all I see is red.

The anger inside of me blinds me, and the next thing I know, I'm pinning Rylan to the wall. My whole body is pressed against him, my forearm at his neck. Growls erupt from behind me, but I'm not fazed.

Rylan, however, doesn't miss a thing. I can feel them move toward us. I can feel their confusion on which one of us to stand up for.

"You touch her, and I'll rip your arms off," he growls, not taking his eyes off me. Our proximity makes his voice vibrate off his body and into mine.

"Why? You want to do the dirty work yourself?" I ask, my eyes flashing. We're both breathing heavily, nearly no space left between us.

"You have no idea what I want."

I don't like the way those words travel up my body. Stepping back, I drop my arms, pushing the hair out of my eyes.

"You can throw insults at me all day, but it's not going to change anything," I say, leveling him with a look.

"You don't honestly believe that you're alpha now, do you?"

Both of us are explosive right now. And irrational. That's a dangerous combination. There's no reason to our emotions. Rylan is clearly panicking, his own alpha wolf in disarray. Just like mine. I'm tired and annoyed and confused and every other emotion I can throw in the mix, but the best thing I am is getting under Rylan's skin.

"What I believe to be true is that clearly *your* alpha wasn't good enough for this pack if the Ancestors decided to award that honor to me."

I fling my words at him, but I want to do so much more. I know I hit him right where it hurts. Anger burns deep within my veins as I try to force air into my lungs.

"Is that what you think? I suppose we'll see how many wolves in *your* pack you'll get killed this time."

Time seems to stop and then restart, except now it moves so much faster.

"You are despicable," I snap, raising my hand to slap him.

But his reflexes are too fast for even me. He catches my wrist, yanking me forward. I fall against his chest, staring up into his eyes. The fire I feel inside me is reflected there.

"Want to try that again, *princess?*" His voice is husky and low. I can feel the rumble vibrating against my chest. Pure anger rises, and I don't hesitate.

Using my body as a weapon, I close whatever tiny distance was left between us. He goes rigid beneath me. I grin, just barely as I spin, using the surprise to get him off kilter before I throw him over my shoulder.

My alpha and his are right at the surface, but this one isn't for them. This one is between us right here and now. He lands on his back but only for a quick second. Soon he jumps up and is on all fours, glaring up at me. He launches his body at me, but I've played this game before. We're equally matched, something he's never been able to be okay with.

I grin as I block his advances, my training coming into play. Jefferson always said a wolf should be able to fight equally as a human and as a wolf. And Jay made sure I could.

Rylan spins around, slamming his arm into my back before I can get out of the way. I topple forward. Instead of stopping the progress, I lean into it, dropping to my hands as I perform a handspring forward. When I land, Rylan is coming for me. I twist my body around, kicking him right in the chest. He slams against the wall but doesn't slow down.

Instead, he pushes off the wall, launching his body at me as he winds his arms around my middle. His sheer size overtakes me, and he slams me to the floor, landing on top of me. His hands pin my arms over my head as he straddles me across the middle. Immediately, all fight goes out of me as I feel him pressed against me.

He feels it too.

Or maybe it's only my imagination. But I swear he tenses as he meets my eye. His eyes move up to my right arm and I see the moment his body language changes.

"What's that?"

I have no idea what he's talking abou. I'm afraid this is just another tactic, but then he sits up, straddling me around the middle as he brings my right arm down in front of me. I see what he means the moment he shows me my wrist.

The white wolf, the outline tattoo I saw in my dream and tried to claw off, it's back on my wrist. The image suddenly becomes clear, merging with the reality of it on my skin. This time, I'm not dreaming.

* * *

EVERYONE IS KEEPING a wide berth when it comes to me, not that I blame them. I would too if I was in their position. I can feel the link to the pack, and I can feel their unrest and fear.

There has never been a female alpha before. There isn't supposed to be one now. I broke the rules, and I didn't even do anything but exist. A part of me wonders if this is what the Oracle was talking about. If this is the way I can help the wolves. Because the only way I can be alpha is with magic. I'm not sure what to think or feel about that.

Rylan and I haven't spoken since we nearly destroyed his house during our fight. The white tattoo also didn't disappear overnight, so I guess it's a permanent kind of a deal.

When the sound of footsteps reaches me, I know who it is before he even steps into the clearing.

Ezra takes a seat beside me, overlooking the valley below. From what I remember, there is a set of caves down there, a place we can go if we ever need to hide.

"I thought it was Zach's turn to watch me," I say, not taking my eyes off the valley.

"You know it's not." There's almost a tone of humor in Ezra's voice, but I must be imagining things. He's not the kidding type. But he is a student, of anything and everything, and he's been doing research.

"What have you found?"

"To be honest, not much. There are no Elders around for us to ask and most of our knowledge was destroyed ages ago in the fire."

I remember the stories of the fire, how humans came in and burned down the village the pack was living in. It's when shifters decided it would be better to keep to themselves. It took years for that ingrained behavior to be reworked. But some packs, like this one, still keep their distance.

"So what do you know?"

"That you're alpha."

I glance at him sharply, but there's no sarcasm or fear in his words. He says them as if they're fact.

"Just like that?"

"Just like that." He shrugs, which is not something I'm used to seeing him do. He usually carries himself more properly than that. I'm not sure why that makes me want to talk to him more, instead of dismissing his words.

"Why didn't this happen before?" I ask, staring at the white tattoo on my wrist.

"Maybe it's like the Oracle said, your vision quest unlocked something inside of you." I glance at him sharply. Clearly, Rylan shared with the class. "Plus, you weren't of age the last time you…were here."

That's true. Even if I was in line to be alpha, the powers wouldn't have transferred to me until I was thirteen. I wasn't even twelve when I was exiled. The pain feels fresh somehow, maybe because I'm back.

"So what do I do with that?" I ask instead of diving into that memory canyon.

"You try to figure out how to work with Rylan instead of against him."

I roll my eyes at that, jumping to my feet. Of course he'd take Rylan's side. I don't know why I would expect anything else.

"If he sent you over here—"

"He didn't," Ezra interrupts, and I narrow my eyes at him as he stands. "From a logical perspective, you both are alpha. Except in your case, you're a step above him. I can't explain it any more than that. This pack will look to him because they know him, but they will look to you because they have no choice. We're bound to you, Trinity. The only way we can make it work is if both of you are on the same page."

I run my hands though my hair, untangling the mess it's become after air drying and then running through a forest. I'll need to get a whole wardrobe and my favorite shampoo and conditioner soon. Such trivial thoughts when I'm supposed to be concentrating on greater things.

"Have you met us, Ezra?" I finally ask, turning to him. "Rylan and I have never been on the same page."

"I'm not sure that's true," Ezra says, walking back the way he came. "One truth I do know is that you have never backed away from a challenge, ever. Not as a young pup and not as the woman who stands in front of me now."

He doesn't follow that up with any nugget of wisdom. He just turns and disappears back into the woods.

Well, I guess I was just kindly put in my place. By Ezra. In his refined gentleman ways. That makes me grin.

CHAPTER 20

Knowing I can't hide on this cliff forever, and refusing to give Rylan the satisfaction of proving him right in that I *want* to hide, I make my way back to the village.

If anyone asks, I will deny it until the day I die, but being back in these woods makes my heart sing a little. Logically, I understand that this is where the blood that pumps inside my veins feels most at home. This is where my heritage lies, where I am the strongest because of the connection I have to the nature around me.

Shifters are connected to the earth in a special a way, something I didn't understand all that well until I had to leave. While we can be happy anywhere, we can only truly thrive in the midst of our ancestors' home. It's why keeping the secret of the village is so important and why we guard our territory the way we do.

That's something I'll have to learn about. The guard

schedules, the different jobs performed by the pack. There are no female wolves here, as far as I can tell. There hasn't been since my mother. And me.

Rylan's mother died giving birth to him. She was the residing she-wolf here, alongside my mom. Dying in childbirth seems to be a curse she-wolves carry. In most packs, mating is a contract. Some pairs do fall in love, like my parents. And Rylan's. But Ezra and Zach's moms were only here, passing by. As far as I remember, at least in Zach's case, his mom went back to the council.

In general, she wolves are rarer and often times treated with reverence. Many of the Elders, from what I've heard, are she wolves. I should've asked the witches if they had any information about that. It would've been an interesting piece of history to learn.

When I step into the middle of the village, I can feel everyone's eyes on me. It would be easy to open up the alpha link and listen in on what they're saying or even feeling. But I don't want to be that kind of a leader.

Because that's what I am.

If someone asked me if I would ever want this position, I would say no. Being an alpha is so much responsibility. Usually, I can only barely manage to take care of myself. But now that I'm here, I want to do the best job possible. I don't want to let the pack down, regardless of how I feel about them abandoning me. They deserve to be taken care of, just like any wolf does. Maybe I can give them something they could never give me.

Jay would say I'm letting my softer side shine. He'd be proud of me. I'm not putting away my tougher side, I'm just balancing the two a little better. The thought of him brings that usual pang of sadness. I wonder what he would think of this whole thing, if he could've ever imagined me as alpha. One of these days, if I survive, I'll have to ask him.

For now, I need to figure out how to coexist with Rylan. So we don't kill each other. Or cause any more damage to the village.

Since I spent last night in the woods, I realize I don't have a house of my own. Pivoting on my heels, I make my way to Rylan's, which is technically the alpha's house. Let's see how he feels about sharing.

I don't knock as I step inside. Three males glance up at me in surprise. Rylan is annoyed immediately, Ezra is stoic, and Zach is trying not to laugh. As usual.

"How cozy," I say by the way of greeting. "I think I'd like to add some watercolors on this wall. How do you feel about ocean views?"

"What are you doing?"

"Figuring out where I'll put my stuff. I really like that clean minimalistic kind of decor, with a few boho references thrown in."

"What even are those words?" Rylan shakes his head, standing. "Get out."

"Umm, no. This is my house as much as it is yours."

"I don't think so."

He looks genuinely perturbed, but I'm not about to make him feel better. Placing my hands on my hips, I turn to face him fully. I don't miss the way his eyes flicker over my dress, but I keep the smile to myself.

"As far as I remember, this house belongs to the alpha of

the pack. Since we seem to share that responsibility for the time being, I believe I am owed my share of the space."

This time, I don't miss Zach's muffled chuckle and neither does Rylan. He throws one look over his shoulder, shutting the beta up.

"Hell will have to freeze over before I live with you," Rylan says, his voice low and dangerous. He truly thinks that tone is going to have the desired effect. I mean, it has an effect, but not one I'm admitting out loud.

"I guess it's a day for miracles because we're living together." I move to go around him, but he grabs me by my arm, spinning me around. If anyone was watching from outside, they'd think we're dancing. The move is fluid and then I'm pressed against him.

"I don't think so." His growl is restrained, but I can feel it against my chest.

"No one is telling you to think."

The words are out before I can stop them, and his eyes flash with the challenge. I can't help but shift my body forward, even though we're already chest to chest. All at once, something rises inside of me. Rylan glances down at my lips, and I fight the urge to flick my tongue over them.

His eyes find mine once again, and then, the screaming begins.

We spring apart, racing for the open doorway before we know what we're doing.

The first thing I see is people running, not in their wolf form, but in their human. Next, I see the rabid wolves.

"How did they find us?" Zach shouts as he races out of the house behind us.

"They shouldn't be able to," I reply, but my voice gets lost in all the screaming. They shouldn't be able to find us. Not when the village is cloaked for this exact reason. The land itself protects us from this kind of an attack.

Unless someone leads them in.

My heart drops as memories assault me from every side. Me, a young pup, caught in the crosshairs as men stepped inside the boundaries of our land.

No, I can't give into it now. I can't let myself fall into dispair. The pack is counting on me to do my part, if nothing else.

Shaking the memories away, I start pulling people out of the way as I race toward the rabid wolves.

"Where are the guards?" I use my pack link to reach out to Rylan, who hasn't shifted yet. He is ushering people to safety. Why is no one shifting?

My question is answered when one of the rabid wolves throws a guard at me. The wolf lands a few feet in front of me, grunting in pain. The poor thing has been mangled, but thankfully, is still alive.

Realization slams into me as I try to pull the wolf to safety.

"We led them here!" I yell, because it's the only explanation. Somewhere during our travels, they picked up our scent, and they haven't let off since.

"Impossible," Rylan shouts back. He's closer now and can hear me without the pack link. The guards are fighting off the wolves as much as they can, but they're still coming forward, down the hill toward us. The direction we came from.

They could've tracked us for that long, but we would've known. Wouldn't we? It's not like there's a tracking device on us.

But then I stop. People push past me, and I nearly stumble as I turn toward Rylan.

"Your bite. They tracked your bite!"

I see the realization on Rylan's face, a split second of emotion, before he shifts, leaping at the closest wolf. Everything is absolute and total chaos.

* * *

THERE'S no hesitation I move toward the wolves, still in my human form. My alpha powers in play, I send a question toward Ezra and Zach.

"Does the underground bunker still exist?"

Zach and Ezra reply immediately, *"Yes."*

"Then get them underground. Now!"

I can feel them moving to obey immediately without question. The underground bunker is mostly a labyrinth of caves. It's the first line of defense. It would lead to the valley where the caves are. That's just another way the earth around us provides for the pack.

Stopping long enough to pull one of the men to his feet, I check him over. Then I send him toward Ezra, who is ushering the pack toward one of the houses where I assume the entrance to the bunker is. The guard is still fighting against the wolves and not making much progress. But I'd rather they hide than fight. Since we have no way to know how the wolves become this, or if it's a type of a disease, I need my wolves away from them. I don't want any of my pack becoming these...monsters.

Without stopping, I shift, throwing my whole wolf body at the rabid wolf in front of me. He was going in for a bite, but my momentum knocks him away.

"Go!" I yell at the guard. He doesn't hesitate to obey. The rabid wolf growls at me, spitting his saliva everywhere before he launches himself toward me again. I meet him halfway. Using my head to slam into his side, he yelps, crashing against a tree. Blood gushes from his head at the impact and then his limp form drops.

My alpha powers are making me stronger than ever before. Since I'm trying not to bite any of the infected, this comes in handy.

I turn to go after the next one when he raises his head in the air, as if listening to something. Then, he howls. The sound is something out of nightmares. It's not a healthy type of howl, but one that seems like it's hurting the wolf, like his lungs are full of blood and his chest is splitting. But the other wolves listen. They all turn, racing into the woods. The closest ones to the fallen grab them with their teeth, carrying them out.

A swift assault and then a retreat?

This makes no sense. I move to follow when Rylan jumps in front of me. I didn't even see him come my way.

"What are you doing?"

"I'm going after them," I reply, as if he's stupid.

"No, you're not."

"Come on, Rylan. You don't actually think I'm going to listen to

you, do you?" Even though we're both still in our wolf form, I can tell he's trying to calm himself.

"You have a responsibility now, Trinity." That sounds a lot calmer than I expected from him as he tries to stare me down.

"No, you have a responsibility. And I have wolves to track. We're sitting ducks here, Rylan. The moment we step outside of the bunker protection, they could be waiting in the wings. I'm not taking that risk."

I move again, but he blocks me.

"Don't make me fight you," I growl, my wolf itching to move already.

"What about the pack?"

I sigh. It sounds strange coming from a wolf.

"You stay here. You take care of the pack. I'll go after the wolves. There's two of us. We can handle it."

Just then, one of the younger men who was passed out on the ground, stirs, gasping as if in pain. Rylan's attention is turned toward him, and I know for a fact he's not going to leave him.

"Do your part," I say before I take off into the woods.

CHAPTER 21

*J*ust like before, there's no scent to follow. I listen as closely as possible, while still moving, to see if I can pick up any kind of footsteps or rustle of leaves, but there's nothing. I waited too long.

Still, I don't stop, continuing to move in the direction they went. I'll circle around the whole village if I have to, just to make sure they're not lying in wait somewhere.

The way these wolves move, the way they seem to think, even in their animalistic brain, it's confusing to say the least. They don't act like a pack, and yet they're controlled by something. I have no doubt in that. The way that one wolf howled—it's going to haunt my dreams. But also, it was clearly a signal but not one that came from him. He was just the messenger.

I start to circle back to the village, hoping to pick up some kind of trail, but it's like they're ghosts. Here one second, gone the next. There isn't even a broken twig on the ground from them.

When a noise catches my attention, I twist around, already growling. But then Rylan steps out from behind a tree. I completely ignore him, but my annoyance is at an all-time high as I turn back to my search.

"Trinity."

"Go home, Rylan. I don't need you."

It sounds harsh, but it's the truth. His presence is just muddling my thoughts as always, and anyway, he has a pack to take care of.

"You're part of my pack."

Now, he's reading my mind, apparently. But no, when I glance at him, he's got stubborn Rylan determination written all over him.

"If we're being technical, you're part of mine."

He huffs but doesn't contradict me. We're never going to figure out how to make it work, not when all we seem to want to do is fight. He stays behind me as I continue my search. It surprises me. I almost expect him to drag me back kicking and screaming. Maybe he's just waiting for his opportunity to pounce.

And now my brain is conjuring up all kinds of other images, and I need to knock it off.

"Trinity, stop."

Here we go. The silence only lasted about five minutes. I shift and turn to him only to find him already in his human form.

"What is your problem?"

"My problem is that you're going off halfcocked to track untraceable wolves by *yourself*!"

This is a new kind of an anger from him and I have no idea how to categorize it. He's nearly mad—maybe a little chaotic—and I don't understand it.

"I can handle myself," I reply, because it's the only answer I got.

"No, you can't. You have to be watched."

He realizes too late what he said. My eyes narrow in response. You'd think he'd apologize, but I know better. Even though he knows he messed up, he doesn't break eye contact. Fine.

"If that's what you think then why bring me back? I know the Oracle told you to," I continue before he can interject whatever crap explanation he had on the tip of his tongue. "But you could've gone against it."

"I couldn't have."

"Yes, you could've. I've read of alpha's breaking a command. It's painful and it's rare, but since I'm causing you so much *distress*, I'd think you would've taken a little bit of pain instead." My voice is full-on dripping with sarcasm, and I'm not even hiding the hurt I'm feeling. Because it doesn't matter. He doesn't see me for who I am, so he should've never even brought me back.

"You think this is a game?" He growls, his words mostly just angry sounds at this point. The laugh that escapes me holds no humor.

"No, I think it's a joke. That you're a joke. You talk this big game about protecting your pack and then you do nothing."

He's right at my face, anger burning the space around me. I don't cower. I don't even flinch. I will never again let him decide my destiny. I'm not a young kid anymore.

"You know nothing of duty." His voice is low, sending goosebumps over my flesh. He doesn't move away either. Once again, we're sharing the same air, the same breath. "You don't understand what it means to sacrifice everything— your wants, your dreams, your desires—for the good of others."

"Don't you dare talk to me about sacrifice." My own words are dangerously low, my eyes flashing up at him. "You have no idea what I've been through. You have no idea what I lost, what I've given up. So don't stand there on a throne of lies like you're the only one who has to make tough choices."

We're both breathing heavily, and I think we've been here before. This is a position we find ourselves in often. We can't seem to stay away from each other, and yet, we're explosive when we come together.

I want to scream at him to understand me, to realize just how much he hurt me when he discarded me like garbage. But I can never make someone else recognize my value, if he's not ready to see it. A part of me wants to reach out with the pack link and see if I can read him, see if I can understand what goes on in that handsome head of his. But I won't. I could never do that to someone against their will.

Instead, I decide to be the strongest of us and I take a step back, inhaling deeply to calm my racing heart. The distance helps but not much. My emotions are still too intense when it comes to Rylan.

"We need a plan. We can't keep living on the defensive.

While my vision quest memories are still returning, we can't just sit and wait for the wolves to attack again. They know where we are now."

Rylan seems to have grabbed control of himself, all business now.

"I assume you have a plan."

I almost smirk in response, "I do. These wolves are careful when they attack, but they have to come from somewhere, right? The town nearby—"

"It's about fifty miles from here."

"But it's close enough that someone might've seen something. Is there anyone of the magical community there?"

"Some, not many. Most moved into more protected communities once the threat of the Ancients came about."

That makes sense. Hawthorne is such a town after all. I spent years there, watching the magical community come together. It feels weird that White Wolf pack doesn't have the same support. But maybe I can find some.

"Okay, then I go. I go research. I find as much information as I can, and you stay here and take care of the pack."

"No, absolutely not."

"I'm not going to disappear or run away. I'm linked, remember? I *can't* disappear. So don't worry, I'm not going to mess up any Oracle prophecies or whatever."

There's that growl again, as Rylan levels me with a look.

"What?"

"You're so clueless sometimes." He mutters the words as he turns away and I don't think I'm supposed to hear them, but I do. I want to call him out on it, but by the set of his shoulders, I think he might be buying into my plan. I don't want to jinx it. So I wait him out. When he finally turns back around, he's back to being the shut-off alpha I've come to know.

"Fine. You go to town, but I'm coming with you. Ezra and Zach can take care of the pack, but you are not going anywhere without backup."

There's no way I'm going to change his mind and standing here arguing much longer just wastes time.

"Fine."

* * *

AFTER WE CHECK on the pack and send instructions to Zach and Ezra, we're off to the town. Both of the boys wanted to come along. Zach seemed to be particularly disappointed. But there's no way we would leave the pack unattended. That's something Rylan and I seem to agree on.

While wolves have no problem protecting themselves, fighting if necessary, this whole situation with the rabid wolves makes it difficult. It's hard to fight them when we can't use our typical methods of biting and scratching. I know Rylan seems to have recovered from his bite, but it's too early to say if it did any permanent damage. We simply don't have enough information. So hiding is what we want the pack to do for now, while we figure this out.

That's step one on my long list of things to do: figure out what in the world is going on. Then, we'll look for ways to combat that.

We shift at the outskirts of town, and I take a moment to tame my flyaway hair. It's mostly wavy with a few curls thrown in where it decides to do that itself. I run my hands through it, untangling it as much as I can and smoothing it out.

When I turn, I find Rylan's eyes on me. They follow the progression of my hands down my dark brown strands, and for a moment there, it feels almost domestic. I'm not sure why that word pops into my head when we're standing in a forest as far away from anything domestic as we can be. But it feels like something one would do, waking up in the morning and getting ready in front of a bathroom mirror.

Wow, my brain is truly losing it, isn't it?

But when Rylan's eyes make it back to mine, that ever-present tension between us heats up, and I'm the coward who looks away first.

The mistrust is still there, even the hate at times, but I could swear something else lurks in his gaze. My own desires want to answer. It's not so black and white between us anymore—it never really has been, has it? But I have no idea what to do about that, and I don't have time to let my mind wonder. There are more pressing problems to deal with.

"I have an idea," I begin as we turn toward the town and step out of the forest. This part always concerns me. If people start noticing that we keep coming out of the woods, someone will start asking questions. Thankfully, Rylan brought us to the back of a bar-type of building, and there are no windows on this side. From what I can see, this is a neighborhood. There are houses with yards farther up the street.

"What's your idea?"

"I think our best offensive when it comes to the wolves is to fight as humans."

"What?" He stops mid-stride, turning to face me. The complete disbelief on his face is slightly adorable, I'm not going to lie. Well, I'll lie if anyone asks. But my wolf and I will know. She seems to like it too.

"Manmade weapons might be our only defense," I say, shrugging. "I know it sounds...sacrilegious somehow, but I don't think we have a choice. We can't fight them the way we fight everything else."

He knows I'm right. I can see it on his face, but he doesn't like it. I can't blame him. Most wolves don't even bother learning human combat because why would they? Their strength lies in their wolf side. Sure, not all wolves are like that—Jefferson's pack being a perfect example. They train as wolves and as humans, and I was lucky to be a part of that. I also happen to know that Rylan, as well as the boys, have trained as humans too. It's something our dads wanted when we were little. I never got to experience it, but I've spared with the boys enough to recognize training.

"You're thinking...knives?"

I miss my knife. I lost it in that first fight with the rabid wolves.

"Or swords, if you can handle it." I wink at him without thought, surprising both of us. He does that stop and stare thing where I think his brain shuts down for a second and needs to restart. It happens anytime I do—anything really. I'm surprising myself by acting like we're no longer enemies. I guess this forced time we've had to spend together is blurring some lines.

"It's worth a shot." Rylan shrugs, and I narrow my eyes at him.

"Why so agreeable all of a sudden? I thought you'd fight me on everything."

Rylan throws me a look that can only described as annoyance before he sighs.

"The survival of my—our pack—is vital. If I have to work with you to make that happen, then I will."

So simple, yet I know how much it hurts him to say those words. They require at least a bit of trust thrown my way, and that is something he never thought he'd give me again. I don't have to read his mind or emotions to know that. It's who we are to each other.

Regardless of who we were to each other as kids.

But I accept what he says at face value. Because just like him, I will do what I must in order to protect the pack. And the rest of the wolves. If I can do something—anything at all —then I will. The Oracle might not have given clear instruction, but that much I do believe.

It takes us about ten minutes of walking through a neighborhood before we step out onto the main street. I give the town a quick study. I remember almost nothing about it from my childhood, and even if I did, I think it would've changed a lot.

Buildings line the road on each side. The setup is very similar to any small town I've been to. Shops line the main road, each building sporting a different color. Flowers are situated down the sidewalk in large planters and hanging off the hooks from the building. Most of the buildings here have a glass front with full displays. It reminds me of Hawthorne.

It holds that small town vibe close to its heart, and I suddenly want to do everything I can to protect the people here.

"Where to? Since you're the human expert."

A couple walking by looks over their shoulders at Rylan and I cover my laugh with a hand. He looks at me confused, and I reach over to pat him on the chest.

"Maybe keep the human versus not human comments minimal? The tourism here is big and you said yourself," I lower my voice, "the magical community is small."

Understanding comes over his eyes before his gaze drops to where I touched him. Removing my hand, I fiddle with my dress a little. I'm definitely reverting back to how things were before the big fall out all those years ago. I need to be more careful. It is amusing to see Rylan here, among so many humans. It wasn't so long ago that I too was a fish out of water—or a wolf out of her woods—among them. I understand how confusing and unsettling things can be, especially if no one has taken the time to teach him about both communities.

"Come on," I say, turning us toward a building far down the street. With my shifter sight, I can see a plaque hanging over the door. "I know just the place to go."

CHAPTER 22

*M*usic and smells hit me before we step inside the bar. The country song is a little too loud, and it's made even more so by the voices that are singing along to it. People are laughing and dancing. There's even an area with a pool table and a dart board. If I was picturing a small-town bar, this is exactly how I'd imagine it. In the corner, there's a pinball machine. Jay told me about those.

As Rylan and I make our way to the bartender, a few people glance toward us. I'm not easy to miss in my bright red dress. Plus, Rylan looks like he just stepped off a runway or out of one of those men's magazines with a lot of buff chests on the cover.

He looks a bit uncomfortable around all these people, and I can't help but smile. Seeing Rylan finally out of his element is something. Not that I frequent these kinds of establishments myself, but I've been around big groups of humans before...and actually have enjoyed myself.

"Hello there, darlin'." The bartender greets me with a smile, and I don't hesitate to return it. The woman looks to be in her late forties with long dark hair braided into two braids. She wears a large turquoise stone necklace. "What can I get ya?"

"Water with lemon would be great," I reply, glancing around the place. Rylan has moved to the other side of the bar, as far away from me as he can go. I don't blame him. I look way more approachable without him around.

"Sure thing. Passing through?" The woman doesn't seem to need to look at what she's doing. Her hands move automatically, finding exactly what she needs before she hands the glass over to me.

"You know everyone around these parts, don't you?" I answer with my own question before taking a sip.

"I do." She's studying me intently, and for the first time, I wonder what other people see when they look at me. The last few weeks haven't exactly been kind to my wardrobe or skin care. Maybe it's silly to other wolves, but I love those types of things. I also love curling my hair and styling it in different ways. That's something the mess on my head could really use right now.

"What are you looking for darlin'?" The woman hasn't taken her eyes off me, even as others are asking her for drinks. There's something in the way she studies me that brings me a bit of comfort. That is the exact opposite of how I usually feel with strangers. She reminds me a little of the

Hawthorne witch's coven leader, Meredith. I've only ever gotten glimpses of her in meetings or talking to Jefferson, but she inspires the same feeling of—comfort.

"Some information, if I'm being honest. I'm wondering if any strangers have passed through here, any...unexplained occurrences going on around town."

Maybe being so straight forward isn't the best choice, but I don't feel any kind of malice from her. Maybe I'm just being naïve, but it's too late now anyway. I can feel Rylan's eyes on me from across the bar. I won't meet them just yet.

"That's a beautiful tattoo you got there." The bartender points to my wrist, and when I glance up from it, I see that there's a gleam in her eye. For some reason, I think she knows who and what I am.

"It's new," I reply. She nods as if she knows it.

"Let me take care of these gentlemen and then we'll see if we can talk."

I don't move from my position, grabbing a vacated barstool instead, and let my eyes wander over the bar.

Rylan is supposed to be doing his own recon, but he's been sitting in the same place, not even talking to anyone. I'm about to open the pack link when someone slides in next to me.

"Pretty girl like you, here all alone?" The guy can't be a day over twenty. He wears the kind of blinding smile all the girls around here must love. I don't give him much, just a polite one in return. "What do you say to a dance?"

I open my mouth to reply when an arm snakes around my waist, pulling me against a tight chest. I don't even have to look to know it's Rylan. He's nearly growling at the guy in front of me.

"She's taken," Rylan says. The guy jumps off the chair so fast, he nearly stumbles. I watch him go, a bit annoyed at Rylan. I would've loved to dance.

"Get your arm off me," I whisper, keeping a pleasant smile on my face. But of course he doesn't. He keeps me firmly pressed into his side, his hand flexing against my stomach. Heat pools at the bottom of it, and I try really hard to keep my breathing level.

"Every guy here wants to get into your pants," Is the only reply I get.

"Well, that's just silly," I say. "I'm not even wearing pants." He growls again, and I can't help but grin. This possessive streak is something else entirely. I think I'm supposed to hate it, but I'm enjoying it? Maybe? I can't tell.

But I do want to dance. I stare at the dance floor longingly, wondering how different my life would be if I could just go over there and lose myself to the song. Rylan finally removes his arm from around me, but he doesn't move away. He leans against the bar beside me instead.

Just then, another guy comes up, and when I meet his eye, he's grinning. Ignoring Rylan entirely, he focuses on me.

"Hi there. I'm Trev. I see you eyeing the dance floor. Would you like to give it a whirl?"

I grin right back because I like the way he asked and the way he holds himself. Jumping off the barstool, I move forward. But then suddenly, I'm being yanked back.

"You should've asked your buddy over there." Rylan's voice is angry and possessive. "But she's taken."

"She is not," I reply, moving forward again. The guy isn't intimidated by Rylan at the least and that makes me grin wider. I reach out a hand for him to take it when Rylan grabs it spinning me around.

"Wanna bet?"

Rylan pulls me in close. One swift yank and my body is flush against his. My breath catches as I register the feel of him against me. His anger is still there, but something else boils under the surface too. I raise my face to his, about to put him in his place, but then he slams his lips against mine. There is no hesitation in me. A storm roars inside of me. And then I can't get enough.

Rylan's hands travel the length of me, taking the bottom of the skirt up over my thighs at the sides ever so slightly, before dropping it back into place. He squeezes my waist, pulling me closer, nearly lifting me off the floor.

I gasp, and he swallows the sound as his mouth explores mine. There's a unique kind of possessiveness in his kiss, a fury that's directed at me, but also not at the same time. He kisses like he can't get enough, like his very being demands our lips to stay together. He devours me and worships me with his kiss and his hands.

My own hands wind into his hair, pulling him down toward me as I inhale him. We're holding each other so tightly, I'm not sure where he ends, and I begin. Nothing in the world seems to matter anymore, as I desperately want to stay in this one moment with him.

It's the laugh that breaks us apart. It takes a moment for me to come back down to earth. I guess Rylan pulled me up because I slide down the length of his body until I'm standing on my own two feet again.

Turning towards the laughter, I see the guy who asked me to dance, a gleam of amusement in his eyes.

"Glad I could help you two clear that up." He mimics the tipping of a hat before he pivots and leaves us standing there. I'm thankful for the bar at my back because my legs are shaking. Rylan doesn't seem in any hurry to move away from me, but I can't look at him. Whatever just happened, it opened up a whole slew of questions and worries and feelings. I am not prepared to deal with any of that right now.

The bartender returns then, motioning for me with only a quick glance at Rylan. I'm grateful for the distraction.

"Come with me."

* * *

WE FOLLOW the bartender to the back office, and once the door shuts behind Rylan, the noise from the bar disappears. I look around in surprise as the woman gives me a kind smile.

"Shifters, right?" she asks, glancing between Rylan and me. We must look shocked because she chuckles. "Don't look so surprised. I know my auras."

"Auras?" Rylan asks, but I know exactly who she is.

"You're a Reader," I say, She points a finger at me, looking pleased.

"A smart girl, you are."

"What's a reader?" Rylan has had nearly no dealings with witches, so I'm not surprised. As far as he knows, they're not to be trusted. That's something that's been taught to shifters for generations. I'll have to tread carefully and make sure he doesn't lose it right here and now.

"A Reader is a witch who can interpret emotions," I begin, taking as step in front of him, which puts me between him and the witch. His eyes snap up immediately. I can tell he's trying to restrain himself. It's an automatic response to meeting a witch and one I also had not long ago. "Some can read emotions clear off you, some can read auras or energies."

"Some can read thoughts and predict the future," the witch adds. At that, I turn to look at her. I didn't think those existed anymore. I remember Jay's girlfriend, who is also a Reader, explained the way her magic works to me. She said that much of the Reader magic, just like with other witches, has been subdued. Her mother is the strongest Reader witch she knows, and she can't read minds.

"How's that supposed to help us? Can we trust...her?" Rylan hasn't taken his eyes off the witch. She chuckles, running her hand over her necklace.

"You shifters, you have such a particular view of witches. Haven't you heard that times are changing?"

"Right now, I don't care if you're a witch. I would ask this question of anyone."

"That I believe," the witch replies. "I'm Stella, by the way."

"I'm Trinity. This is Rylan."

Stella looks between the two of us, a small smile on her face. I wonder what she's picking up from our auras. I'm always aware of him, his nearness. Right now, he seems to be standing even closer than usual. And after what happened in the bar—no, I'm not going there. I'll have to figure out my confusing emotions later. Right now, we have a mission.

"Well, Trinity," Stella begins, keeping her eye on me. "You wanted information on odd occurrences. Why is that?"

I don't reply right away, thinking through how much to tell her.

"*You can't tell her anything.*" Rylan's voice in my head makes me jump, and he glances over at me in question. For some reason, I thought he'd keep the link closed off until we were able to have a conversation about what happened. But honestly, his stern command just makes the decision for me.

"We're tracking rabid wolves," I say, meeting Stella's eye. Rylan groans beside me, turning away from the conversation as if it pains him. I ignore him. "We have no idea what's causing wolves to disappear and reappear with none of their human side intact. Have you seen any of that around here?"

"I have." For some reason that surprises me. I wait for her to go on. "This town doesn't have much of a coven or a supernatural presence at all. We did, once upon a time." She looks somewhere beyond my shoulder, as if remembering. "But now, I'm one of the few that keep these people safe. The Ancients didn't use to care about the humans, but they do now."

"What do you mean?" Rylan asks from behind me. I'm glad to see he's paying attention.

"All I have are rumors, but I've heard human factions have been forming. There are groups who know about magic users but are in support of the Ancients' agenda. And the Ancients are taking note."

"This doesn't make sense," Rylan says, almost to himself. I

risk a glance at him, and he looks pretty disturbed. My emotions must still be jumbled from that kiss because I have a pretty big desire to go to him. That needs to stop immediately.

"It's not unheard of. It has happened before."

"What do you mean?" I ask, turning my attention back to Stella.

"You know the story of the Ancients, right?"

"Yes."

"No." Rylan says at the same time, and this time, I'm not really surprised. It's the witches who keep records, the ones who know the lore, even though it's been passed off as fables for generations.

"I mean, I know some," Rylan continues. I feel him move to stand beside me.

"Just like the majority of the magical world." There's a kind smile on Stella's face, and I can't be sure, but I think her tone puts him at ease.

"I will give you the condensed version. Eons ago, so long in fact that there are no definite records, the Ancients roamed the earth. Harsh and prideful rulers, they battled for power and for magic. They experimented on living things, creating the first witches and shifters. When they exhausted themselves in such a way that they could not sustain the world anymore, they went to sleep. For generations, they slumbered.

"A few years ago, they began rising again, reawakening their magic and their ambition. But what most don't know, is that through the years, the Ancients have appeared—waking up long enough to work their ways, before going back to slumber. Not many people saw them, but enough did that the worship of these creatures became a secret society of sorts. A secret so buried in the human world that none of the magical community knew about it until recently."

As Stella finishes her story, all I can do is stand in place, frozen. I knew about the Ancients. I came from a town where the number one goal was protecting its borders from the Ancients so they didn't get to the powerful nexus at the center of it. But to know that Ancients have walked the earth before, and recently enough to create human allies—I don't know how to take that.

"Do you mean there some of those people here in town?" Rylan appears to be better at processing, I guess, as he asks the question. Maybe it's because of his previous mistrust of humans. Or maybe he can compartmentalize better.

"I think there are. I have not been able to find out one way or another, but I've had my suspicions. Either way, there are a lot of shady groups in town, some who frequent this establishment."

"Is there a way for us to find out for sure?" I ask, finally finding my voice.

"Honestly, I fear that they know about you already, and they'll find you before you find them."

"Is that a premonition?" Rylan asks. There's no sarcasm or hatred in that question.

"It might as well be, Rylan," she replies. I can feel, rather than see, him stiffen beside me at the casual use of his name. This is probably the first time he's talked to a witch like this. A part of me is proud of him for opening up to the possibilities.

Shaking my head, I put those feelings away and focus on the issue at hand.

"I think if they don't know we're here yet, we should make them aware," I say. I can tell Rylan doesn't like my plan just by the way he growls, but it's the best one we got. We need to figure out what's going on.

CHAPTER 23

*W*hen we step back into the bar, it has cleared out significantly. In fact, there's only about fifteen people in the whole place. The music has been turned down some, but it's still loud. Rylan's body grows rigid next to me because he's picking up the same energy I am—which is danger.

"Are these the shady characters you were talking about?" I ask as the witch walks out to stand beside me.

"Unfortunately, yes."

"I guess we don't have to go looking, huh." I say.

"The rats brought themselves out into the light."

There's hardness in her voice and determination. I can't imagine how hard it must be for her to protect this town nearly by herself. But we're here now, and I'm not about to let these men walk out of here without getting some answers.

"Who do we have here, Stella?" One of the men steps up,

giving Rylan and I a once-over. He's clearly supposed to be the leader of this little group. He's dressed in a button-down and slacks, instead of the t-shirts and jeans the others are wearing. He leans against the bar, reaching for a glass and downing the contents in one swig.

"You are not welcome here," Stella replies, her voice hard.

"We're not leaving until you tell us about your guests."

"Or you can talk to us directly," I snap and take a step forward, only to feel a hand on my upper arm. Now Rylan is the one holding me back. I glance at him, and he opens up the pack link.

"We have to be smart about this."

"We have to fight. You and I both know this."

These men didn't come here to talk. I can tell that at a glance. I'm not exactly sure what they want, but we're not simply walking out of here. To be honest, it'll be nice to do something besides run around this whole country looking for answers. It's been a while since I've gone hand to hand with someone and given it my all. My limbs could use the stretch.

"You're a tough pretty thing, are you?" the leader says, now addressing me. "I think my superiors would like to meet you."

"Oh, so you're not the top dog? Why am I not surprised?"

The man narrows his eyes at my dig. Rylan growls beside me, his hand squeezing tighter on my arm.

"Trinity, there are fifteen of them."

"Don't tell me you're afraid of a little tussle." I glance over and Rylan's mouth goes up at one corner, his eyes shining with anticipation. He's into this, just like I am. If I'm being

189

honest, I'm kind of excited to see how Rylan fares in a human fight.

"Watch your mouth, wolf. Before we shut it, permanently."

Well, that answers that question. They know what we are. That means we'll have to be extra careful, in case they have anything up their sleeve. It's time to stop playing this stand-still game and get started. I glance over at the witch and she gives me a tiny nod.

"Just try not to break my whole bar," she says. The leader's eyes snap over to her. I feel pressure in my left hand, as she pushes something into it. The heavy weight of a handle settles into my palm comfortably.

"What did you just say?"

"She said," I turn his attention back to me. "Don't make him bleed all over my beautiful floors."

These men carry enough ego that those words are all it takes. They attack as one, separating Rylan and I immediately. I throw the knife Stella gave me into the air, and catch it mid fall, slamming it straight into my attacker's collarbone. He screams, stumbling. I kick him into the two coming forward, sending them flying. Glancing over, I see Stella in the corner, fighting off one of the guys. Her moves are fast and sure for someone who doesn't really practice violence. But I suppose all of us do what we must in order to survive.

Another guy comes around the tables, winding back for a punch. I duck just in time. He swings again, and I use two arms to block him before I grab that arm and twist it behind his back. I yank down hard enough to break bone. He hollers, and I use his moment of distraction to grab his head and slam it straight down onto the nearest table.

Another man replaces by the one I just took out. I dodge his punches, left then right, before ducking under his arm and ending up behind him. I push him forward with my leg, and then grab a chair.

"Hey there," I say as he turns. Then I smack the chair across his face. He goes down with a satisfying crunch.

Before I can drop the broken chair, two guys descend on me. One grabs me by the hair, yanking my head back, as the other punches me straight in the stomach. I slump over, forcing my lungs to inhale. I hate that Jay was right about fighting with my hair down. It does give my attacker an advantage. Oh well, live and learn.

As I bend over, dropping against the table, I can feel the guy come behind me. So, I push up on my hands and drive my legs straight back into him. He falls backwards, landing between tables and chairs. I jump on top of the table as the other guy tries to grab me. In a flash, I kick him straight in the face. He's knocked out completely, which makes me grin.

But of course, pride comes before the fall, because I'm grabbed around the ankles and yanked down hard after that. I slam down on the table with a yelp, my shoulder popping out of its socket. The scream that rips from my throat is involuntary as pain radiates all over my body.

I hear a roar and turn my head to see Rylan's full attention on me. The madness in his eyes buzzes. Anger pulsates off him in waves. He picks up the guy in front of him, throwing him like a bowling ball into a set of pins. The man's limp body slams three men into the back of the bar. He doesn't hesitate to punch the next one coming to him, one, two, three times before grabbing his head and slamming it down against his knee.

The guy next to me reaches for me, as if he's going to pick me up, but Rylan is already there. He holds the knife I dropped and stabs my attacker with one upward motions. The knife slices through his kidney. The man drops immediately as Rylan yanks the knife back out.

"I think you dropped this," he says, moving into my personal space.

"Ah, how thoughtless of me," I grind out, but the pain is too much. I'm sweating. I try to see past Rylan, but it's clear all the attackers have been taken care of.

Stella is suddenly there, looking down at me.

"You had your bell run, darlin'," she says, then looks at Rylan. "Take her upstairs. There's a room to the left. You can stay there while I clean up this mess."

I move to sit up, but Rylan's arms are around me and he lifts me into his before I can protest. I still do though.

"I can walk."

"Sure." But he doesn't put me down. I pull my hurt arm over my stomach, cradling it against me so it doesn't jar. I feel tired. It's probably from having my head slammed down so hard. Instead of being proud, I rest my forehead against Rylan's chest. He says something to Stella, and she replies, but a weird noise begins at the back of my skull and moves forward.

I refuse to give into the blackness, so instead, I focus on Rylan's heartbeat against my cheek. It's much too fast.

I don't realize I say the words out loud until he chuckles. I don't think I've heard him laugh since I've been back. It's a nice sound.

"Thank you."

Crap, I'm saying my thoughts out loud. I need to shut up. He chuckles again, and then he's carrying me away.

* * *

BEING CARRIED by Rylan feels kind of like floating. Maybe it's my concussion talking—I'm almost one hundred percent sure I have one—but his grip is firm yet comforting somehow. He's so big that he can cradle me against him without jarring as he walks up the stairs. I didn't even know there was a staircase here, but I guess Stella showed him where to go.

The ceilings here are lower and the light is dimmer. I stare up at Rylan's chin, so defined it can probably break bones. I wonder if he used that chin in the fight just now. I'm stuck with the sudden urge to laugh because why would he use his chin to break bones when he's got these powerful arms of his?

They feel strong around me now, but they felt even stronger when he held me to him at the bar. When he kissed me senseless. My skin tingles from the memory, my body coming alive with that one thought.

Rylan groans, deep in his throat, his whole body vibrating with the sound.

"If you don't knock it off with those thoughts, Trinity, we'll both be in trouble." I can barely make out his words over the roughness in his voice. I duck my head deeper into the crook of his arm, but that doesn't seem to help at all.

I feel him open the door when a swift gush of air passes. He then walks into an even more dimly lit room. Depositing me onto the bed with a gentleness I don't expect from him, he takes a step back to study me. I'm still holding my arm against my chest, since that's the only position that doesn't bring excruciating pain to my shoulder. It's out of its socket, that much I can tell.

If I breathe too harshly, it sends pain down my body.

Rylan steps into the doorway and returns a second later with a glass of water. I glance around me and realize we're in a room big enough for one bed, and that's it. The bed touches the walls on either side, making this more like a little box than an actual room.

"Here." Rylan hands me the water. I take it with my good arm, but even that seems to be too hard right now. He grabs the glass before I can drop it, bringing it gently to my lips. His other hand cradles the back of my neck, just barely, as I tip my head back to take a swig. His entire concentration is on my lips and the water, so I get to watch him over the rim of the glass without him noticing. I take a few sips, before he guides my head back into a neutral position.

"You know I have to reset it," he says, still only a few inches from my face. I give him a tiny nod. I can feel my body wanting to heal, but my shoulder needs to be corrected before it does.

"Have you done it before?" I ask as Rylan sets the glass of water on the floor.

"I saw it on TV once." My eyes fly up to his, and I'm

shocked to see a tiny smile on his lips. With just that small change, his whole face transforms. He's always been gorgeous, but like this, he looks like the guy who was my best friend. The one I would've done anything for.

"I'm kidding, Trin. I've reset plenty of shoulders."

It's the nickname that gets me. My eyes fill up before I can blink the tears away. Rylan's face drops and then he's kneeling beside me.

"It hurts that bad? Do you need me to see if Stella can get you something?"

"No, I'm okay," I reply, not meeting his eye. This is a side of him I never thought I'd see again. The caring sweet alpha, who wanted nothing but to protect me. We were only kids, barely even teenagers when I was exiled, but I remember the thoughts and feelings I was starting to develop for him. Ones I thought were gone forever. And now, I don't know what to think.

"We need to do it soon," he says. I nod again. Because he's right. Closing my eyes for a moment, I push the tears down and turn to him. His face is a lot closer than I expected. My breath hitches at the proximity. His eyes flicker down and I almost lean forward, but then he stands.

He doesn't go far though.

"You'll need to scoot back a little." He guides me back until the back of my knees hit the bed. Then he steps right into my personal space, taking my arm from where I've been holding it. He stretches it out to the side without moving it up, as if he knows exactly how far to raise it before he hurts me. One of his knees come between mine as he kneels on the bed. His other leg rests on the outside of mine. I hold myself as still as possible while he places one hand under my armpit.

I've seen this done before. I know that people sometimes use their legs to stabilize the shoulder and it's done laying down. But Rylan is so big, he has no need for that.

He leans forward, over my shoulder, his breath ruffling my hair. His fingers travel the length of my arm to the wrist, positioning it in a straight line. There's a moment of stillness. The sensation of his skin against mine races over my body and then he pulls.

One swift yank, I yell, and then it's over.

He steps back, placing my arm down. I move my shoulder a little to assess the damage. It feels back in place.

"Thank you," I say, looking up at him.

"You're welcome," he replies, not taking his eyes off me. There are so many things I'd like to say to him right now, but my head feels heavy, and my eyelids close on their own.

"Trinity, don't fall asleep." Rylan is beside me as my body leans back into his arms.

"I don't want to," I reply, right as I pass out.

CHAPTER 24

When I try to open my eyes, the light is too bright. I squint against the blinding intensity, trying to figure out where I am. I can tell that I'm standing, but I'm almost positive I was just laying down.

As suddenly as the light appeared, it disappears. I find myself in the middle of a meadow. Spinning around I see nothing but a sea of dandelions. They surround me on every side, the flowers taller than I'm used to, coming up almost to my waist. This has to be a dream, but I don't remember falling asleep.

"That's because you didn't."

I turn at the voice, finding myself face to face with a giant white wolf. Her fur is glowing from inside, the fur moving gently in the breeze. I'm shocked at the sheer size of her, and suddenly, I feel like I'm experiencing déjà vu.

The wolf watches me patiently, as if giving me the time I need to process what I'm seeing and feeling. It feels almost like a memory that's been overshadowed by others. The image is right there—but I can't seem to reach it. A sudden stinging sensation makes me glance down at my wrist. My eyes latch onto the mark I now carry there. Looking at it, my brain seems to restart. I look up at the wolf in surprise.

"You were there during the vision quest. You came to me."

"I did. What do you remember?"

"I remember you coming to me." I concentrate hard, pushing the fog away to find the memories. "You told me— you told me to be true to myself."

"I did."

"Is this what you meant?" I raise my arm to show her the mark. She glances at it briefly, but I swear she smiles.

"It's part of your journey."

"And what's the other part of it?"

"Ah, always so eager with questions. That part you'll have to discover for yourself as well."

The enigmatic way she speaks, giving away nothing, is truly annoying. There has to be a way to get something out her beside half answers. Actually, I wouldn't even call them half. They're like a one percent answered questions.

"If you're supposed to be my spirit guide, you're not giving much guidance," I point out, folding my arms in front of me. This time, I'm sure she smiles since her eyes crinkle at the corners.

"You'll have all your questions answers soon enough."

"Is that in a time measurement for normal people or magical ones? Because I've learned those two are not usually the same length."

The wolf nods her head, making a small circle around me.

I turn with her as she walks, afraid that if I look away, she'll disappear.

"You are smart, Trinity. The alpha in you is strong."

"You knew." I suddenly realize it. "You knew about this alpha situation. Why didn't you warn me?"

"Maybe I did. You don't remember much of our conversation. And some of it, you will never remember, even as your memories return."

"What do you mean?"

She has made a circle around me, stopping in the same place she appeared. She doesn't answer right away, as if she's choosing her words carefully.

"When the time comes for you to remember, there will be a piece that is missing. As if you heard the words, but they were spoken in a dead language. This is for your own protection. All of this." I think she means the dreams, "is to protect your mind. Learn about your mark, about your powers. And you will understand why things must be the way they are."

"Are you telling me these dreams are here to protect me?" I can't quite grasp what she means by that, but she nods.

"Yes."

Okay. So I'm processing information, but it manifests in dreams? Does that even makes sense? But it must. Since I'm doing it. This is so frustrating! Everything in my life has become a crazy jumble of magic, confusion, and Rylan.

Now I'm thinking about Rylan.

The way he tasted, the way he felt.

The wolf in front of me makes a noise and I glance up to find her watching me with a gleam in her eye. I can't quite tell what she's thinking, but I almost think she knows what's going through my mind. There's no harm in asking, I suppose.

"How does Rylan come into play?"

She doesn't reply right away. She watches me for a long moment, before turning away.

"Wait—"

"Come back to this safe place when you need it, Trinity. I believe in you."

And with that cryptic farewell, she's gone. Like she was never even there.

If this is a safe place, it should be less confusing.

WHEN I OPEN MY EYES, I'm laying down, and the ceiling above me doesn't look familiar. Turning my head to the left, I see that I'm not alone. Rylan sits at the end of the bed, his back to me.

I give myself a moment to study him before I let him know I'm awake. From this angle, I can almost see the heavy weight he carries on his shoulders. I've only been alpha for two days, and I can already feel the responsibility nearly crushing my heart. He's carried that with him for years. It's why he didn't hesitate to summon me back, even though I know it's the last thing he wanted. Because he would do anything for his pack. I understand that now.

As I push myself to a sitting position, the bed shifts and he turns. There's a moment where his eyes hold me completely captive before he reaches forward to offer assistance. I don't think I can handle touching him right now, so instead, I use my hands to push off and slide forward on the bed until I'm sitting next to him.

"How long was I out?" I ask, running a hand through my hair. My shoulder throbs a little, but it's a manageable pain, mostly just soreness.

"A few hours," he replies. "Stella came by, brought some food." That's when I notice the smell. I look over as he hands me a brown paper bag. Inside, there are chicken strips and chips. I reach for them immediately.

"She also said the downstairs is secured, she had to run an errand and she's opening up in a few hours. I have no idea how the whole witch thing works."

Rylan sounds genuinely confused, and I nearly chuckle. I don't think he'd appreciate me laughing right now, so I eat my chicken strips instead.

He grows quiet then, and the only sound in the whole building is my chewing. So sexy.

No. No. No.

Not that it matters what I sound like.

I'm definitely getting more and more annoyed at myself by the hour. Everything I know and feel about Rylan is jumbled. That kiss definitely rattled my nerves. And I really need to not be thinking about that right now when he's barely two feet away. I stuff another piece of chicken into my mouth instead.

"I've also checked in with the pack. They're still underground and there haven't been any other attacks."

I nod, since my mouth is full. For a second, I think Rylan is going to smile. I really should know better. His eyes move down to my lips and then he stands abruptly. I swallow my food before speaking up. I think he wants to pace, but there's not much space in this tiny room.

"I remember more of the vision quest."

He pivots at my words, his attention once again on me. "It's not much, but there was a white wolf there. I think she's my spirit guide. She said that something big is coming, and it'll be up to me to make a decision."

"That seems incredibly vague."

"I think it's supposed to be."

I heard somewhere that people have a tendency not to want to know their future. They say they do but not really. Because then their every decision, every move, has this shadow hanging over them. Is this the right decision? What if the other move was the right one? Maybe that's what the white wolf meant when she said she can't tell me, and that my brain needs to process how it will process. My decision must be my own if I'm going to make sure everyone survives this.

It seems like an impossible goal, but one I will work very hard toward.

"I've been thinking, if we can't track the wolves, can we track the humans from downstairs?" Rylan breaks through my thoughts. I look up at him, only for him to look away. His cagey attitude is making me a little crazy, I'm not going to lie. He's acting like an omega, not an alpha.

Finishing off my food, I put the trash away and stand. My head still feels a little heavy, but the rest has given my body time to heal. I don't say anything right away though, waiting until Rylan looks me in the eye. It takes a good minute, but he finally turns his attention to me, narrowing his eyes.

"What?"

"Nothing. Just waiting to see how long you're going to act like a little boy."

"Excuse me?" He looks entirely too shocked at my audacity, and that's more like it. I let my lips curl up in a smirk.

"You're excused. Now, let's go track some humans."

I move past him, but he catches me by my good arm, pulling me back against him. My back slams into his front, and his other hand wraps around my stomach, pinning me in place.

"You shouldn't talk to me like that." His words are a barely audible growl in my ear. It sends a million tiny goosebumps all over my body. That angers me more than his body against mine. I reach for his thigh, digging my fingers into it. Then I let my body go limp against him. Every cell in my body is fully aware of how he feels against my back, even through layers of clothing. He pulls me in even tighter, as if I'm going to slip out of his grip. He teeters on the edge of control. When his head drops forward into the space between my head and my shoulder, he inhales. Just as much in a battle with himself as I am with myself. We're on uneven ground, neither one of us knowing what to do. So of course, I do the only thing I can. I grab his arm, yanking it away from my stomach, as I drive an elbow into his.

He stumbles back, mostly because I've taken him by surprise, since I don't use any real force behind it. He lands in a sitting position on the bed. His eyes are full of anger and hunger, as he looks up at me and I can't help but grin.

"I'll talk to you any way I want," I say before I turn on my heel and walk out of the room. I don't get far. He's in the small hallway in a flash, pinning me against the wall.

"You play a dangerous game."

"And you don't?" I fire back, raising my chin. That, of course, brings our faces barely a few inches apart. I know he's thinking about that kiss. So am I.

"If you think you can simply manipulate me because of that kiss—"

"Oh, so we *are* acknowledging it," I interrupt. "Just a reminder, you kissed me."

"And you didn't push me away." He's quick with a retort, his eyes flashing. Fine, two can play this game.

"I was a bit stunned by the unskilled way you handled me. Should we get you to take some lessons?"

His growl vibrates across my body as his knee wedges itself between my own. Now there's no space left between us.

"You're just lying to yourself."

"Is that what you do? Pretend everything away, until there's nothing left but this hard shell of a man."

Maybe I'm being too harsh, but I can't stop the hurt that's piling into my heart or the desire that's nearly shaking my body. Who was I kidding thinking Rylan and I have reached some kind of a milestone. It's not even about the kiss but the fact that we were working together—that he took care of me. I'm too jumbled in my head.

"What? Nothing to say?"

"You have already made up your mind about me," he replies, taking a step back. I miss his heat immediately. "Wouldn't want to ruin a pretty picture you painted in that head of yours."

He doesn't wait for a response, simply turns and jogs down the stairs. I give myself a minute to calm down. His reaction is so uncharacteristic to the typical confidence he displays, I don't know what to do about it. The tirade of emotions he brought so close to the surface make me want to scream. But I don't. Because I shouldn't care how Rylan feels about me. There's no future where we're anything but reluctant allies.

And that's fine by me. Five by five as dad used to say.

Five by five.

CHAPTER 25

*W*hen I make my way downstairs, Rylan is nowhere in sight, but Stella is behind the counter. She looks up as I enter, giving me an encouraging smile.

"How much of that did you hear?" I ask, and she chuckles.

"I don't even need to be a Reader to know you two have explosive chemistry between you."

"I wouldn't call it that."

"What would you call it?" She hands me a glass of water, and I take it gratefully, leaning over the bar.

"A time sensitive partnership."

"Mmhmm."

She watches me as I down the water. Then I hand the glass back. She continues to polish glasses as she moves down the bar. I give it a quick glance around and see that everything looks normal.

"How did you manage this?"

"A little magic. I cast a restoration spell while you were fighting, to protect you and this place. Your injuries could've been much worse, especially where you hit your head."

I look at her in confusion. "I don't even remember hitting my head."

"Exactly. That's the most dangerous kind of wound, the one that you don't see coming."

For some reason, I don't think we're only talking about my head here. I glance toward the exit, knowing I need to go after Rylan. I could reach out with the pack link, but I don't think I'm ready for that yet. Honestly, I could probably use some distance from him right now. Our emotions are way too heightened.

I focus on Stella instead.

"The men who came here, they seem to know you."

"I told you I've been noticing things. It's because this is a one-of-a-kind bar in town. Everyone comes through here."

"Do you know where they operate out of?"

She studies me for a moment, putting the glasses down and leaning on the bar.

"Don't tell me you're about to do something stupid."

"I'm always a step away from doing something stupid," I reply, grinning. "It's mostly research. We need to know what they're up to."

She waits another beat before she gets back to work.

"I honestly cannot tell you where they operate from, but I can tell you that a fifteen passenger white van showed up here a few hours ago to pick up those who were still walking, and those who were not, and drove off north. I haven't been able to find their location, which leads me to believe they're cloaked from my magic. But I doubt they're cloaked from yours."

"I can track them."

"I think you can." She reaches under the bar before placing something on top of it. I look down and see it's the knife she gave me earlier. Blood covers the blade. "I think this will help."

I could hug her right now. She pushes it toward me, and I take it carefully, ready to ask if she needs it. But she's already two steps ahead.

"I took some of the blood, just in case. And the knife is yours to keep." She produces a sheath next, a dark blue one that will wrap nicely around my upper thigh. "A woman should always have multiple secrets."

"I like the way you think," I reply, taking the sheath and pulling my dress up over my thigh. With my leg up on the bar stool, I wrap the strap around it, liking the feel and the look of it. A noise catches my attention and I look up to see Rylan frozen in the doorway. A spark of electricity passes between us as his eyes move from my thigh to my eyes. I give myself a second to feel it all before I drop the dress back into place and turn toward Stella. The witch wears a knowing look on her face, but I ignore it and pick up the knife.

"We'll let you know what we find."

She grabs my left wrist, the one with the amethyst bracelet that is still miraculously intact.

"I know you can handle yourself." She lowers her voice, and I think that whatever she's about to say is meant just of me, "And so can he. But you need each other. It's okay to ask for help sometimes."

She let's go of me then, straightening, and I take two deep breaths before I turn away and head to the door. Her words repeat in my head as I step out into the sunlight.

* * *

RYLAN and I don't talk as we head in the direction the van took earlier. I keep the knife hidden in the folds of my skirt, but I can't keep carrying it like this.

When we pass an alleyway, I grab Rylan by the hand and pull him with me. He comes willingly, which kind of surprises me, but whatever. I'll deal with that later.

I hand him the knife. He takes a good sniff before he hands it back. I do the same, and then I pull my skirt up. Rylan freezes for a moment, and I can't help but roll my eyes. Sometimes, he's such a guy.

With the weapon secured and the skirt back in place, I look back over at him.

"We need to shift. We'll track faster that way."

"There's an alley that borders the forest on the next street over."

I mull that over. I don't want to leave the direct route, but we do need to get out of town. I'm pretty sure two giant wolves wandering around Main Street is going to raise some serious red flags. So I nod and wave my arm in front of me, for him to lead the way. He does.

At least we understand each other's cues better? I'm not sure why I feel the need to look for a silver lining in all this, but here we are.

It doesn't take us long to reach the alley, and when I do

shift, I stretch my limbs out a little. It feels good to be back in this skin, especially after my injury. The rest of the residual pain disappears as the healing becomes complete.

Grateful for the witch's magic that makes sure my shift kept the knife on me, we begin to run. Our senses are heightened, and it's easier to pick up the trail.

It leads us straight out of town and away from our village. A part of me is thankful for that. It would suck majorly to have the bad guys residing next door to us. Rylan doesn't say anything, but I think he's relieved too.

Speaking of the pack, I should probably check in on them. But I don't think they'd appreciate that like they do with Rylan. Even though most of them knew me when I was young, they didn't choose me as alpha. It feels awkward to be the one to reach out to them now. So I simply trust that Rylan did and everything is fine.

We don't speak as we run, but I know he keeps the pack link open. It's kind of crazy how I can feel that now, since we can both open the link. Regular shifters have to rely on the alpha to do so, but we don't.

After another hour, when the sun is setting, we finally hear noises of civilization. There's a dirt road off the main highway, and we keep to the shadows of the woods as we follow it.

When we come to the end of the road, we stop, both of us unable to describe what we see.

It's a compound, of sorts. There's a large fence all around it. I can tell it's electrified, even from this distance. There are guard towers spread out enough that every vantage point is covered. Rylan and I take an automatic step back farther into the woods.

Past the fence is a building. It's large from what I can tell, and we only see the front portion of it. The back spreads out into the forest. I can't tell if the forest continues or if it only takes up part of the building.

"How do we get closer?"

"I don't know if we can."

We stand there a moment longer, trying to think. Eventually, Rylan speaks up again.

"Let's see how far this goes."

I nod and follow him as he begins to circle the compound. We go for miles before the fence finally curves. Sticking to the cover of the forest is tricky because it takes us farther away from the building. When we meet it again on the other side, the sun has set.

"This compound is huge. I have never heard of such a place anywhere around these parts."

"Stella said it was cloaked from her magic. Maybe it's cloaked from humans too. What would they need this for? What could they possibility be doing in there?"

"I'm not sure, but I can tell you that I don't want to find out firsthand." There's a note of worry in Rylan's voice. I follow the direction of his gaze until I notice a gate previously hidden in the fence opens up. A van drives out, much like the one Stella described, but it doesn't head toward the road. It heads in the opposite direction.

There's an opening in the woods farther down, and Rylan and I don't hesitate to follow. We keep our distance. My heart beats faster and faster as the van drives farther. Finally, it stops.

We come around through the trees, and I see that it's parked in front of a cave opening. Maybe it's a mine. The van doors open, and two men get out. They walk over to the back, both carrying sticks. Once the door opens, something between a growl and a howl sounds from inside. One of the men points the stick inside, and I hear the unmistakable sound of electricity striking something. The sounds of pain intensify, and then one of the men grabs a chain and yanks on it.

My heart drops in my chest as a man steps out of the van. Except he's not fully a man, part of him is wolf. He's a mixture of both, as if he got stuck midshift. He looks like he's in pain as a guard yanks him by the chain toward the cave opening. Once near there, the guard reaches into his pocket and takes out something that looks like a syringe. He sticks the man quickly and efficiently. The man drops to his knees, yelling as his body ripples in the midst of a shift. He still doesn't change, but he slumps down to the ground in a heap. At first I think they killed him, but then I see the barely-there movement of his chest. The other guard brings another man, who looks the same, out of the van and follows the exact process the other did. Once both of them are there, the guards step back all the way to the van. The first man takes a small object out of his pocket. He places it against his lips and blows.

Even with my supernatural hearing, I can't hear anything. But then, I hear a growl.

A wolf, one of the rabid ones, comes out of the cave. He

looks at the two men lying on the ground, then at the two standing by the van. I think for a second that he'll leap onto them, but he doesn't. He turns his attention back to the fallen men, bends down and picks up the chains with his teeth. Then, he drags the men into the cave.

The two men by the van wait a full minute before they get into the vehicle, turn around and head back. I can't seem to move. Not toward the cave nor to follow the van back. Rylan nudges me with his nose, but I've got nothing. I'm in complete shock.

CHAPTER 26

"*Trinity*."

It's the alpha voice, but it's gentle. It finally pulls me away from my thoughts. I look over at Rylan and see the same despair I'm feeling all over his eyes.

"*We have to move. Before they know we're here.*"

He turns to go, glancing over his shoulder to make sure I'm following. I am. I'm moving now.

We race through the woods, a straight line away from the cave and the compound. I would've loved to have explored further, but we have to be careful now. Extra careful.

When we're nearly back to the town, Rylan slows down. I've been running on autopilot, my mind processing everything we saw, everything I picked up. Rylan finally stops, turning around to face me as he shifts. I follow suit, and then I sit right down in the damp earth, face in my hands.

Fear and anger shake my body. I think I might explode. So many thoughts race through my mind, so many questions.

When I feel Rylan reach for me, I don't hesitate to fall into his arms.

He's taken a seat beside me and I fold into him as I try to force air into my lungs. It feels the same as how I felt in the shower, a near panic attack, thoughts jumbling together and yet, I have no control over my body. My hands shake as I pull them away from my face. One of the fists curls into Rylan's shirt.

I don't cry.

No, this is not the time for crying. I cannot give in to that feeling of helplessness or I'm afraid I won't be able to pick myself back up.

Rylan's thumb traces circles on my lower back. I focus on that one spot, on that one sensation, using it as an anchor. There's a part of me that wants to stay in this moment forever, safe and secure. It's strange to think that I could feel like this again with Rylan, but this is a glimpse of the boy I knew. And because I opened up that train of thought, I let it in.

When we were kids, Rylan and I would disappear into the woods for hours. Sometimes, when we were supposed to be at lessons, we would sneak away and basically play hide and seek with our teachers. Being two years older than me, he sometimes taught me the lessons I would receive at the village, since he'd been through them already. My dad was notorious for collecting information, and he passed it on to me in stories.

Rylan would make those stories into adventures. He was carefree and excited about life in a way I've never seen from anyone else.

When our parents disappeared, Rylan shut down completely. I tried to be there for him, but he was the alpha. At fourteen. He couldn't run through the woods carefree anymore. He had to make the tough choices. And then he made a choice that broke my heart.

I don't want to think about that right now, but the hurt is there. Yet, comfort is there too. With his arms around me, my panic recedes.

After what seems like hours, I finally feel stable enough in my own skin to even raise my head. When I do, I'm met with a storm of emotions in Rylan's eyes. I can't tell if he's remembering, like I was, or simply processing what we've seen.

"You realize what they're doing, don't you?" I whisper, afraid to even utter the words, but I know they must be said. "You felt it, right?"

"Yes." Rylan's voice is gentle, but anger simmers right there near the surface. "There was no wolf in them, just human."

"They're taking humans and experimenting on them, just like they're taking wolves. I—it makes no sense. Why would they do that?"

My mind tries to put together the pieces, everything we know, and everything I've remembered from the vision quest. From the dreams I've been having. None of it fits together. It's like I have all these pieces, but they're all from different puzzles. How do I make them fit when they're not even meant to be on the same table?

"I don't know, Trinity," Rylan finally says, sighing deeply. "But this answers some questions, especially why we haven't been able to find them. They're taking them and feeding

216

them to the wolves. And there's a magic there. I don't quite know what kind, but I felt it."

"I did too." I stop for a moment, thinking it over, "I don't think they're feeding them though. I think they're still alive, just stuck in that state, which has to be excruciating."

We're both silent for a moment, grieving the lost souls those wolves and humans are. Once again, Rylan and I have found common ground. I just wish it wasn't freshly dug graves.

"We have enough to start looking for answer," I say, pushing the hair out of my eyes. "There must be someone—" I stop, straightening. An idea forms, something I should've thought of earlier, especially after the mark appeared on my wrist. "I know who we can ask."

* * *

"You want to go to witches for help?" Rylan looks at me like I've lost my mind. We're back at Stella's bar, and in the back room, the one that's, apparently, magically soundproof. Stella stands near the door, listening but not interrupting.

"What do you want me to do? We can't figure this out on our own. We'll be running around all over creation, trying to fight off the attacks but getting no closer to any answers. They can help."

"I don't trust them." Of course he doesn't. Seeing what humans are doing to the wolves hasn't exactly helped the cause. But I'm not giving in on this.

"Well, I do. So tough luck."

"I'm not going to stand for that. They're witches."

"You know there's a Latin term for how you're acting." He looks at me like I'm crazy. "I believed they called it *jerkasa-mongus*." I grin at him just to drive the point farther, and I swear Stella is holding in a laugh at this point.

He growls at me, but doesn't protest further. He wants to, that much I can see. I feel like him arguing with me is his security blanket now. It's where he feels the safest because I know I can't explain what's going on between us. We go from hot to cold to freezing to burning. It's not exactly an easy thing to figure out.

"Stella, back me up here." I turn to the witch, but the older woman simply raises her hands.

"Sorry, darlin'. I ain't getting in between pack business. And I'm partial to witches, so my opinion wouldn't be unbiased."

"At least you admit that," Rylan grumbles. I roll my eyes. Now he's definitely acting like a little boy, and instead of hugging him, I'd like to spank him. His eyes snap up to mine as if he heard my thoughts out loud. There's nothing childish about him now. He's all man in that one look. I think my face might be on fire. It's a good thing the lighting here is so dim.

"On that note…" Stella's voice is full of amusement. When I turn to her, there's a twinkle in her eye, which makes me blush harder. "You can stay upstairs in the room. It's cloaked from outsiders and will be a safe place in case they have a way to track you. You can use my computer right over there." She points to her desk, and I can see a laptop sticking out from under a pile of papers. "I'll do what I can on my end to find some information as well."

She steps forward then, reaching for my hand and giving it a quick squeeze.

"You have a good heart, Trinity. I know you will find answers."

She smiles over my shoulder at Rylan and then she opens the door, letting in the sound of the bar before it closes behind her and it gets quiet again. I can't tell if her words were a wish or a premonition, but I'll take both, at the same time.

Now, I get to call Hawthorne. I probably shouldn't be this excited in light of everything that has happened, but I am.

Walking over to the computer, I turn it on, pulling up a video calling app as I sit down. But then I think better of it. Maybe sending a text first will work better. I memorized both Leah's and Harper's numbers when I was in Hawthorne, and I'm grateful Jay made me do so. He doesn't have a phone, or I would've texted him.

The texting app is on the computer as well, so I put in the number and then a quick explanation of who I am and why I'm contacting them.

"You're one hundred percent sure this is a good idea?" Rylan asks over my shoulder. I turn just slightly to look up at him.

"I am."

Before either of us can say anything else, the video calling app rings. I know it's Leah's phone from the number. I click answer and the face of my friend fills the screen.

"Trinity!"

"Leah, hi." And then Jay is there, squeezing in next to his girlfriend.

"Trin! Look at you. How are you? What is this about disappearing wolves? Jefferson came back telling me nothing. I've been so worried about—" He stops as Rylan steps forward, a low growl at the back of his throat. Jay's eyes snap up to the alpha and then down to me. "Is there something I should know?"

"You should know," I turn and literally push Rylan a few steps back, "that I have a lot of questions."

"Okay," Leah says, petting Jay on the arm before turning to me and giving me a serious look. "What do you need?"

CHAPTER 27

*a*fter I've explained everything that's been going on, Leah said she'll take Harper and Jay to the coven's library and search through the ancient texts. Jay stays hovering in the background, his eyes mostly on Rylan the whole time. I wish I could hug both Jay and Leah but at least seeing them soothes my heart a bit.

Once we're off the video call, Rylan and I head upstairs. We've been going pretty much nonstop for two days. Well, except I had a mini nap when I was recovering from that concussion. So, we're both tired.

When we step inside the tiny room, I realize there's only one bed and there isn't even room on the floor for anyone. We stand side by side in the doorway for a moment before Rylan motions me forward.

"Just take the bed. I'll be fine."

"You will," I reply. "Because it's big enough for the both of us." I point to one side and then to the other. There's no way I'm letting him sleep on the floor while I take up the whole bed. It's huge, wall to wall. We could probably fit another body in between us.

"Trinity—"

"Don't argue," I sigh, turning to step into the bathroom. "I'm too tired to fight you on this." And then I shut the door. Everything about this bathroom is tiny. I don't think Rylan could even fully fit in here. I use the bathroom and then wash my face and arms. The cool water feels nice against my skin.

My dress has definitely seen better days. I'll need to get a new one in the morning. I'll attract too much unwanted attention in this. Unhooking the strap from around my thigh, I place it on top of the tiny counter. Taking the knife out, I clean the blood off, since we don't need it to track anymore. After I wipe it clean, I put it back in the sheath and leave it on the counter.

I study myself in the small mirror, and I'm surprised to see that I have changed. It's not much, but there are lines of maturity around my face. My cheeks are a bit more defined, my eyes sadder somehow. I can feel and see the weight on my shoulders. Glancing down, I study the wolf mark on my wrist. It hasn't faded a bit, still just as shiny and white as when it first appeared. I asked Leah about it, but she didn't know anything. It would be nice to have an answer.

I hope I get something to go off of. Their library is one of the most stocked in all the magical community. They've been the keepers of magical knowledge for generations. It's just another reason why the town of Hawthorne is so important to the Ancients. There's knowledge there they missed while they slumbered and won't be able to get anywhere else.

Pulling my hair over my shoulder, I begin to braid it as I step back into the room. Rylan has taken off his shirt and boots, laying down on top of the covers. He stares up at me for a second. His eyes follow the movement of my fingers as I braid. When I'm done, I have nothing to tie it with, so I tuck it up into the back of it, so it'll stay well enough as I sleep. He watches me still as I take off my converse and then as I scoot back in bed. We lay like that for a moment, side by side, as I stare at the ceiling, and he stares at me. I think he wants to say something, maybe clear some of the air between us. But then he stands abruptly and heads toward the bathroom. I watch the muscles in his back tighten right before he shuts the door.

I can't even imagine what's going through his head. I'm not sure I want to know anyway. When we were kids, he shared his every thought with me. Now, I'm scared of what he'll say.

Pulling the covers up, I slide into them. The cool fabric feels nice against my skin. I feel bad for laying down in my dress, but no matter how immodest shifters usually are, I can't do that in front of Rylan. I just—can't.

Turning away from the bathroom, I face the wall and wait for him to come out. When he does, I close my eyes, breathing slowly to appear asleep. I probably can't fool him, but this saves both of us from having to say anything. When the bed dips with his weight, I become instantly aware of just how close he actually is. The space seemed bigger before we were both in it.

Maybe that's something I need to get used to. Rylan and I seem to take up room no matter where we are. The two of us together become something else entirely. I can't explain it, but the idea tastes true.

I think I'm too aware of him to fall asleep. I can feel his body heat reaching out to me, and I focus on his breathing. For some reason, the combination of his head and his breathing soothes me. Before I even know it, I'm asleep.

* * *

A KNOCK on the door pulls me from sleep. I thought I'd dream, but there was nothing. When I open my eyes, I realize I'm plastered against Rylan, his arm around me as he sleeps. I jerk to a sitting position, almost smacking myself against the wall, but he catches me in time, holding me in place.

"I don't bite. Unless I'm asked." His eyes are still closed as he delivers the line. I'm grateful because I'm sure I'm the same color as my dress right now. The barely-awake Rylan is something else. I think he's forgotten who he's in the presence of.

Scrambling off the bed, I head for the door, smoothing my dress out. Stella is on the other side, a smile on her face.

"Good morning, you two. You have a call. And there's breakfast downstairs."

"Stella, you are amazing." I reach over, giving her a hug. She returns it as if she needs it as much as I do. I step back inside the room, grab my shoes and then I'm down the stairs before I even put them on. I need to put some distance between Rylan and me. Waking up in his arms felt a little too good.

"Harper, hi," I say as soon as I see who's on the screen.

"Hi, Trinity. You really know how to stir up trouble, don't you?" She says it with a smile and I take a seat in front of the laptop, pulling on my shoulder.

"You know me, addicted to the dramatic."

"Well, my dramatic girl," Jay appears on screen beside Harper. "We have a lot of information to share with you."

"I knew you would."

I had absolutely no doubt they'd come through. I feel Rylan before he appears on the screen behind me. My skin buzzes with awareness, but I keep my attention firmly plastered to the computer. A cup of coffee is placed in front of me. I look down at it in surprise before I look up at Rylan.

"Don't read too much into it," he grumbles and I try not to smile.

"I wouldn't dare."

When I turn back to the screen, Harper is smiling and Jay is frowning. Okay, anyway. Focus, Trinity. You have wolves to save.

"Okay, tell me what you found."

Harper launches into a brief history of the Ancients, emphasizing the parts involving shifters. This is all information we already know, but then she says something that completely baffles me.

"You're actually telling me not all Ancients are evil?" I

can't believe what I'm hearing. That has to be false. Our whole history—the history of the world—is built on the fact that they are.

"It's a recent discovery, but I think it may be the answer here," Leah says, stepping into frame as Harper gets up to move. I can see Jay hovering in the background, a worried look on his face. Every so often his eyes shift to Rylan and the worried look is replaced with dislike. I'm trying very hard not to smile.

"How so?" I force myself to focus.

"The first shifter, the one who started it all, there's a chance he might be able to help." Leah continues, placing a book in front of her. "If you can find him, you may be able to figure out what they're doing to the wolves. But Trinity, it's not just the wolves any more. I checked with Meredith this morning. She's been keeping it quiet but we're getting reports of other shifters experiencing the same effects. This is much larger than we thought."

I let that sink in.

"What about this?" I raise my hand, showing them the tattoo. "Any information on this?"

"The only white tattoos mentioned in the sacred texts are about true alphas. But we don't have much information here. Jefferson is checking with other packs, but—"

I've already stopped listening. True Alpha. Just like the Ancients, I always thought that was only a story. I can feel Rylan's gaze on me, and I finally meet his. What I don't expect to see is the complete awe in his eyes. It's only there for a moment, but I catch it, and I think I'll be seeing that look in my dreams.

"You know what that is?" Leah asks. I turn my attention back to her.

"I only know what my father taught me as a kid," I say. "A True Alpha is supposed to be one who leads multiple packs, one who's chosen by the land and the blood and the magic."

"Isn't that all alphas?"

"No," Jay replies, coming farther up to the screen. "Alphas are a blood heritage. It's been told that a True Alpha possesses magic, a healing touch, or something else, I'm not sure. I haven't heard the story since I was a pup."

Glancing down at my wrist, I can't help but feel it, the fact that what they're saying is true. It makes sense why the wolves reacted the way they did, why the pack—my pack—had no control over it choosing me. The land did that for them.

"If what you're saying is true, then maybe the whole prophecy the Oracle had is possible. I can help the wolves."

I wish the texts we used to keep at the village were available, but everything was destroyed in a fire with only oral stories to keep the knowledge alive. And when there are no Elders around to tell those stories, everything gets lost.

"Trinity." Rylan's voice breaks through my thoughts, and I turn to look at him. He's taken a chair and has been sitting quietly next to me during this whole exchange. There's too much in his gaze for me to decipher. And now is not the time.

"Leah, is there any information on where the first shifter may be?" I ask, tearing my attention from Rylan's imploring eyes and back on my friend. She shakes her head sadly, but I also see the way her gaze flickers between the alpha and me.

"There's a lot of speculation. Could you ask the Oracle? Is that something she would be able to guide you on?"

"Honestly, I don't know." I shrug, thinking back to the strange woman and her half truths. "She speaks in riddles or doesn't speak at all. Our last conversation didn't exactly provide answers."

"But maybe," Harper says from over Leah's shoulder where she's been reading something.

"What?"

"Maybe the vision quest she performed, maybe it unlocked whatever it is inside of you that was guarded. You've never displayed alpha powers, not for as long as you were with Jefferson's pack, right?" The last part is directed at Jay, and he shakes his head.

"No, Trinity has always been strong, but that was from hard work. I trained her every day, and she showed up with her whole being."

The growl that emits from Rylan is barely audible, but I hear it. It sends a rush of goosebumps over my skin, but I try not to let it show. He's doing his possessive thing again. I love and hate it at the same time.

"So if you never displayed those powers, maybe they were dormant," Harper continues, completely oblivious to my inner turmoil. "And the quest unlocked it somehow."

I think back to it, how I can only remember a very small portion of the conversation but how I remember the white wolf now.

"The white wolf," I say, and everyone's attention focuses on me. "What if she's the true alpha? And she chose me."

Everyone seems to hold their breath as they let that sink in. Then, it's Jay who leans toward the screen, his eyes intensely on mine.

"Then, Trinity," he says "You be the woman I know you are and you do what is required of you."

CHAPTER 28

$\mathcal{I}$'ve been pacing for the last two hours. After we hung up with the Hawthorne witches, all the information they shared has been spinning around in my head.

True Alpha.

Possible magic.

Not all Ancients are evil.

It's too much to process. I need something tangible to do. And I can't stop thinking about that compound and those wolves.

Rylan is checking in with the pack over the link, making sure they're still fine. Staying in the bunker is probably their best bet until we return. He's not going to like it, but I need to go see if I can find out more information about that compound.

When I turn, he steps through the doorway. I'm in Stella's office, since I wanted to stay close to the laptop in case the witches called back. The bar is getting loud again, as the patrons make their way inside after work hours.

"Whatever you're thinking, don't," Rylan says. He pins me in place with his heated gaze, and I can't seem to look away. We've been so unbalanced since coming into town. Fighting and kissing and sleeping in the same bed. I don't know where I stand, and I don't know what to do about that.

"If you're reading my mind, then you already know what I'm going to say."

"You want to go back to the compound."

I'm not even surprised he can see right through me. Probably because that's exactly what he wants to do as well.

"We need more information," I say. "Our number one priority was to figure out a starting point. Well, now we have two. The humans in this town and on that compound are not going to stop until we force them to, but we can't do that until we know what's actually going on. While the witches do more research, I think it makes sense to go back and see what we can dig up."

"It's dangerous."

"When has that ever stopped us?" I can't help but grin at him. He blinks and I think he knows exactly what I'm referring to. When we were kids, we would take all kinds of risks, just to see if we could. The way his eyes watch over me, I know for a fact he hasn't changed in that regard.

"Fine. But it's only recon. We're not getting involved. Not yet."

"When did you become so cautious?" I ask, moving toward the door.

"When I was thrust into responsibility I was not prepared for."

I freeze, and so does he. Clearly, he didn't mean to admit that out loud. But the raw tone of his voice makes it evident that it's a truth he's been guarding for years. For the first time—ever—I think about how being alpha at thirteen must've affected him. That kind of crushing responsibility is difficult for any shifter to bear, and so much more so when it's put on someone before they're ready.

"Well, now we share it, right?" I'm not sure what possesses me to say that. I think he's going to protest or get defensive, but he watches me curiously instead. Maybe we're finally coming to terms with our responsibilities, with where we fit in. Then, he simply nods and turns toward the door.

I follow him out, passing a few people as they head toward the dart board.

"You're heading out," Stella says as we stop on the other side of the bar. It's not even a question, as if she's been expecting this.

"We are."

She leans toward me before she speaks. "This bar is protected. If anything happens, get back here as fast as you can."

I nod and then thank her before turning to Rylan. We leave the bar behind, heading toward the woods. A few people glance our way, and I realize, I really need a new dress. This one is way too noticeable in its disarray.

Once in the woods, Rylan and I don't hesitate to shift. We race through the forest, not bothering with conversation. My heart beats so fast, I think it'll beat right out of my chest. The closer we get to the compound, the more nervous I get. I can't tell if it's just my nerves or if it's something else. Like the magic in me, sending off warning alarms.

Now I'm overthinking everything. Just because True Alphas supposedly had magic, doesn't mean I do. Figuring that out is an item to add to my to-do list for later. Right now, I need to figure out if we can get inside the compound unnoticed.

"Should we circle again?" Rylan asks when we reach the woods on the outskirts of the compound.

"I'm not sure that'll do us any good." I look around, trying to find any weaknesses in the fence. The only entrance I see is the main gate and the side gate where the van pulled out earlier. I head in that direction before I speak over the link. *"Maybe if we wait long enough, they'll do another run."*

Rylan doesn't argue but settles in between the trees, his eyes trained on the gate. I'm a little surprised he's taking my lead this easily. I'm used to him fighting me every step of the way.

"If you're expecting an argument, you're not going to get one." He doesn't look at me as he speaks through the link, and I send a glare his way. I don't like him reading my mind like this.

"You're way too agreeable all of a sudden," I say.

"Just trying to keep my pack out of trouble."

That makes sense, I suppose. I keep pushing him, and he keeps protecting me. So maybe it's just easier to go along for now. It's his duty to the pack that's keeping him here, it has nothing to do with me. I'm not sure why I want it to.

I think I'm about to say something I'll regret when the

door at the compound begins to lift. Rylan and I both stand immediately, our shifter senses spreading out around us as we watch the van pull out.

Before I can think too much of it, I take off running toward the closing door.

"Trinity!"

Rylan's voice is in my head, but I don't pause. The cover of the setting sun is on my side. Everything blurs around me as I push to go faster. Right before the door shuts, I slip beneath it, Rylan right beside me.

"Are you out of your mind?" His eyes are wild. He looks like he's ready to throttle me.

"Now is not the time," I throw right back at him. "Let's move."

We stay close to the wall, keeping to the shadows. The courtyard stretches out in front of us, toward the building in the middle of the closed off area. Instantly, I notice the cameras in the corners.

"Trinity."

"I see them."

This was a terrible idea. We're pinned in place, because if we move forward, they'll see us. And there's no way out.

CRAP.

I shouldn't have been so reckless. Glancing over at Rylan, I find his attention on our surroundings. He's processing, just like I am. Before either one of us can come up with an answer, an alarm blares. The sound is ear shattering, and I whine involuntarily. My body seems to fold in on itself. I can't make my limbs work. This isn't a normal sound, but a specific one for the wolves. The people in this place have done their research.

"We have to move. Trinity. We have to—"

I can hear Rylan's voice, full of the pain I'm feel in my own body. Even though we want to move, we can't. I walked us—no, ran us—straight into a trap. It's like they baited us with that van. It came out way too fast after we got here.

The door opens on the building closest to us. I twist my body as much as I can to see three men step outside. They're carrying the same type of Taser device as the men in the van.

I struggle to stay upright, my wolf going absolutely insane inside of me. She's feeling caged, even though she's out, and I can understand that all too well. The men reach us in the next moment. An electrical shock slams into me. I howl, my body shaking as I drop down to the ground. Rylan's howl follows my own, the pain shaking every cell in my body.

"You didn't actually think you could get in here so easily, did you?" One of the men snickers, leaning down toward me. "We know everything that goes on in these woods."

That's impossible. But maybe not. If they have magical help on their side, they can track us that way. With human advancements, like the cameras, they have yet another way to keep track of everything.

I was so stupid to think I could just waltz in here without a plan.

The electrical shock comes ones more, nearly blinding me from the pain. All of this is a lot more complicated than I thought. My own actions have brought us here, and now Rylan is going to die because of me.

No, I refuse to give into that train of thought, even as I grind my teeth together to keep from screaming again. I can't give them any more satisfaction.

"Hold them down," the man says. Rough hands grab me, pinning me down. Wiggling my body side to side, I try to get out from under their grip. But between the siren blaring and the electrical shock, I'm too weak. I feel a pinch and then something is inserted into my shoulder.

"Make sure to get more blood than that," the voice says as I try to clear my mind.

"It's hard to break through the fur. I don't get it—"

"Just do it already. They're not going to be like this forever."

The men continue to argue as I focus on my wolf. She's panicking and I need her calm. This whole situation is manageable. We can get out of here. I know we can.

My eyes find Rylan, as he twists on the ground under the hold of two men. I see a syringe extracted from his fur, as he howls in pain. Seeing him like that, completely helpless, does something to me.

The pain recedes. It's still present, but my attention is diverted to Rylan. A longing rises up inside of me—to protect. With every fiber of my being, I want to protect him.

A howl rips out from somewhere deep in my soul. I jump up, and in the same moment, the men tumble away in shock. I don't hesitate to pounce.

Landing right on top of the closest man, I push him straight into the ground. Another man tries to reach for me, but I dig my teeth into his shoulder, and then he's the one who's screaming. Tossing him into his colleague, I turn to the man near Rylan. The growl that rips out of my throat brings even more fear into their faces. They can't tell, but I'm grinning.

My body moves before I think too much of it, pouncing on them. They try to stab at me with the Tasers, but I jump out of the way. Then my claws dig into one of the men's back. He stumbles forward. I grab another man by his side, flinging him across the courtyard.

"Rylan, get up."

The other alpha doesn't move. For a second, I panic. But, no. I can feel him. He's just frozen.

"Rylan, get up. Now!" There's my alpha voice—the command echoing inside of my own head too. Rylan's eyes snap up to mine, clearing enough that he jumps to all fours. There's more shouting, more people running toward us.

If we don't get out of here now, we're never getting out.

My eyes zero in on the men, and that's when I see it. They all carry a keycard around their necks. Racing over to one man, I yank a keycard off with my teeth before I rush to the gate. Shifting to my human form, I swipe the keycard against the reader on the wall. At first, nothing happens. But then the gate begins to lift.

"Let's go!" I shout, and Rylan rushes through. I shift, just as the men reach us, before racing back out into the forest.

Shouting reaches my ears right before the sound of gunshots erupts.

"Don't run in a straight line!" I scream, weaving from one side to the next. Humans and their human weapons. That's

something else I didn't think about when I ran head first into the open gate.

A bullet passes right between Rylan and I, making my heart drop. We're way too close to the compound still. I don't think we can outrun them.

"*We have to lose them in the trees,*" Rylan shouts. I agree. But how? They're right on our tails. "*We need to separate.*"

"No. Absolutely not. Head for Stella's but stay to the trees," I reply, a plan formulating inside my mind.

"*What are you going to do?*" Rylan's voice is full of worry, as if he once again can see inside of my head.

"*I'm going to keep them occupied.*"

I turn my body away from the forest just as Rylan shouts.

"*Trinity, no!*"

"*Yes. Go to Stella's.*" There's that alpha command in my voice. I see Rylan's body shake from it, as if he's trying to fight it. But I guess I do have more power than he, because he has no control over himself as he rushes into the forest. With one last look after him, I pivot and race back toward our pursuers.

CHAPTER 29

*T*here's no hesitation in me as I turn toward my attackers. All I can think about is protecting Rylan. Protecting my pack.

Being pushed into the whole alpha situation wasn't something I ever would've wanted for myself. But just like at the village, a feeling of belonging washes over me when I think of the pack.

Maybe that's what the white wolf meant about me being true to myself. I have always been protective of those I care about. Shutting off that part of me would be—wrong. So I'm going to do what's right.

My wolf is ready to take on whatever comes her way, which makes me grin. I feel strong and powerful, more so than I have ever felt in my whole entire life.

The van screeches to a halt in front of where I stand in the middle of the clearing. Rylan has to be halfway to Stella's by now, and that gives me comfort—knowing he's safe. Four men jump out of the van, this time with guns in hand.

"You should've ran when you had the chance," one of the men says, raising his gun in front of him. He holds it carelessly, as if he feels absolutely no threat from me. When I shift into my human form, he takes an automatic step back. He didn't expect that.

"What exactly do you think you'll accomplish here?" I ask, my voice clear. The sun has set, and the only light comes that from the compound. Luckily, with my shifter eyesight, I can see the way the men shuffle uncomfortably. Maybe they're not used to seeing the magic of the shift so naturally.

"We're bringing in the next era of the world!"

"Shut up," the other man snaps, glaring at the one who spoke. I'm not surprised though. There's something about people like this, those who are willing to do the unthinkable. They like to brag.

"A new world order, huh? That sounds exciting." I know I'm egging them on, but I need to make sure Rylan is back at Stella's. I need their full attention on me.

"You have no idea."

My eyes drop to the gun for a moment before meeting the man's gaze once more.

"Are we just going to stand around, or are we going to fight?" I say, cocking my head to the side. "Don't tell me you boys are scared of a little girl."

The front man raises his gun again, ready to fire. I think if I shift now, I might be able to attack. But I don't get the chance to find out. A blur of white comes out of nowhere, dropping straight on top of him.

Rylan.

Anger and fear grip my heart, but I can't let him fight alone. One of the guys is on me before I can shift. He raises his hand holding the gun, but I knock it away. Then I kick him in the groin. As he bends forward, I knee him in the head. He drops as another man swings at me. We're in close combat now and I don't hesitate to put my whole body into the movement.

Spinning around, I slam my elbow into the man's back, pushing him forward. As he tries to find his footing, I spin, swiping his feet right under him. He lands hard, and then I'm shifting. Rylan has taken care of the others. We have a window to get away and we take it.

Racing into the forest, we move faster than ever before. This time, we don't stop or pause for anything. We're in town before I know it and stumbling into Stella's bar, which is full of music. Her eyes find us immediately. We must look terrible because she's not the only one who has noticed us.

Motioning us toward the back, Rylan and I step inside her office, shutting the door behind us. The moment it shuts, I turn on him, slapping my hands against his chest hard enough to send him backward against the door.

"What were you thinking? I gave you a command."

"What was *I* thinking? Are you crazy? I wasn't going to leave you!" he snaps right back. We're both breathing heavily, but not from the run. From fear.

"I gave you a command."

"You need to work on your alpha voice. It didn't do much."

"You could've been killed."

"Yes. But guess who was in more danger? You!" He's right in my face, but I'm not backing down. "You have got to stop putting yourself in these situations. You are not alone. You are not disposable."

"Don't tell me who or what I am."

His words make me panic, because they sound almost—almost like he cares. So of course I go on the defensive. Adrenaline is still pumping through my veins, my head and heart full of Rylan and the way he's looking at me right now. We move closer to each other, as if we're being pulled together.

"You are alpha. I see that now, Trinity. Maybe that's your purpose, maybe it's something else. But you can't keep putting yourself in danger like that. You can't."

"Isn't that what an alpha does?" I ask, my voice dropping a few notches as I take another step toward him.

"Give me a chance to have your back," Rylan replies, closing the remaining distance between us. There's so much weight in that one sentence, I'm not sure what to do with it. But then, I don't have to do anything.

The door opens and Stella steps in.

"Oh good, you're done screaming at each other," she says giving us a knowing smile. I step away from Rylan, running a hand through my hair. "What happened?" Stella asks.

"I was reckless, and I almost got us killed," I reply. I see no reason to beat around the bush.

"Okay, so you do better next time."

My eyes fly up to meet hers at the words. There's no judgement behind them, just a truth. The emotions racing through me are making everything jumbled.

"It's not that simple."

"Sure it is," she says. "You wanted a starting point, right? Well, now you have multiple. Decide what you're going to do with all the information you've collected and go from there. You have someone who will listen and process that information with you." She looks over at Rylan before opening the door back up. "I got you both new clothes. You can change upstairs."

With that, she opens the door and steps back into the bar.

I still feel guilty, but she's right. We haven't stopped the rabid wolves or the Ancients or even the humans at that compound. But we finally have something we didn't have before. Information. Our first step was to find a starting point. No matter how bad things got, at least we completed that first step.

* * *

HOURS LATER, after the bar has closed, Stella, Rylan, and I sit around the table in the main room. We've changed out of our dirty clothes, and I, at least, have calmed down some. Becoming alpha has made my whole world spin off its axis. Finding my footing is going to take time, but I can do this. That's a new kind of calm.

The witches and Jay said they'd keep us updated if they find anything else. They have their own worries with the Ancients, but they told me once that I was family, and they're treating me as such. They'd do anything for family.

"I'll get us drinks," Stella says, standing. She pats my shoulder as she passes. We got her up to speed as much as possible, but she won't interfere with our decision making. The men at the compound seem determined, and now they have our blood. I'm not sure how to feel about that, or the fact that I basically handed it over to them. We have to figure out what to do next. That part is up to Rylan and me. Before we make any decisions, we need to check on the pack.

"Are you ready?" he asks. I want to say no, but I nod instead. It's the first time I'm using my alpha powers across so much land. A normal wolf wouldn't be able to do this, but it's the special gift of an alpha.

Rylan reaches across the table, offering his hand palm up. I stare at it as if I've never seen a hand before.

"It'll be easier to stay linked if we're touching," he explains. I see no other choice. Flexing my hand a little, I place it into his. The immediate awareness of our touch is there, and I feel it in every inch of my skin. Our eyes meet, and for some reason, I think he can feel it too. He nods, and then we open up the link.

It seems weird, they're miles away, but I can immediately tell they're underground, still following the command I uttered. Rylan looks at me, as if encouraging me to be the first one to speak. Seeing no other choice, I do.

"*Ezra.*" I call on the beta and he responds immediately.

"*Trinity. Are you alright? Rylan?*"

"*Yes, we are both fine. But we have found some disturbing news. We'll be coming home soon, but for now, I need you to watch over everyone for a little while longer.*"

There's a moment of silence and then, "*Is there anything I can do?*"

"*You're doing it by keeping them safe,*" I reply. I think he can feel the honesty in that one phrase. We might not be friends yet, but I think I have earned an ounce of respect from Ezra, and I hold onto that.

"*Understood,*" he finally replies.

"*Thank you,*" Rylan says. I can feel a thrill of joy from the others at hearing his voice. He has built a strong relationship with the pack, that much is evident.

"*You are welcome,*" Ezra says.

With that, Rylan and I shut off the link, but he doesn't let go of my hand. My chest is heavy with the emotions I picked up from the pack. Most of it centers around fear, and that hurts my heart.

"Is it always like that?" I ask, glancing down to where Rylan's thumb now makes small circles against my hand. I've figured out his trick by now. He does this when he can tell I'm starting to panic. I won't call him out on it because I don't want him to stop. It centers me, even though I won't admit that to him right now.

"Sometimes it's lighter, sometimes it's heavier," Rylan replies honestly. I'm grateful he's not sugarcoating it for me. Stella returns then, placing glasses of water and some chips in front of us. She glances down at our joined hands, yet, I still don't pull away.

"Have you decided what you're going to do?" she asks.

I shift my attention to Rylan, meeting his eye. We may still be at odds ninety five percent of the time, but we know what we have to do. He followed my lead blindly in those woods and it got us in trouble. I'm not about to make that mistake again. With everything we know, everything we've been able to find out, there's really only one option at this point.

Finding the first shifter is going to be nearly impossible and probably more dangerous than anything we thought we'd ever experience. Going straight to an Ancient when we've spent our whole lives fearing them—it's going to test us in ways we can't predict.

But I know that no matter what, Rylan and I will do this. And we'll do it together. He nods his head, just a tad, as if he can read my thoughts and agrees with every single one of them.

With his hand still holding mine, I look up at Stella and smile.

"We're going hunting for an Ancient."

SEE what happens in next installment, Wolf Untamed!

NEXT IN THE WHITE WOLF SAGA

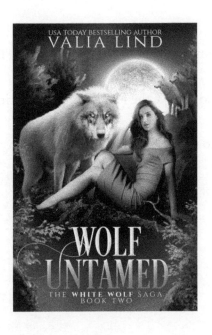

Trinity and Rylan take the fight to the Ancients in the next installment of the White Wolf Saga!

If you love fast-paced action, enemies-to-lovers romance, snarky heroines and broody heroes, then you'll love Wolf Untamed, the next book in a pulse-pounding series by USA Today Bestselling author, Valia Lind.

Thank you for reading my book! If you have enjoyed it, please consider leaving a review. Reviews are like gold to authors and are a huge help!

* * *

They help authors get more visibility, and help readers make a decision!

And, if you'd like to stay up to date with all of my shenanigans, sign up for my newsletter today!

You will also receive the FREE prequel to Trinity's story!

You can find the link readily available at https://valialind. com/free-book/

Thank you!

MORE FROM THE HAWTHORNE UNIVERSE

If you'd like to learn more about the Hawthorne universe, including the witches and shifters at the town Trinity stayed in, you can check out three complete series:

Hawthorne Chronicles
Thunderbird Academy
Faerie Destiny

Find out more information at http://valialind.com

ABOUT THE AUTHOR

USA Today bestselling author. Photographer. Artist. Born and raised in St. Petersburg, Russia, Valia Lind has always had a love for the written word. She wrote her first published book on the bathroom floor of her dormitory, while procrastinating to study for her college classes. Upon graduation, she has moved her writing to more respectable places, and has found her voice in Young Adult and cozy mysteries.

ALSO BY VALIA LIND

The White Wolf Saga

Shared Dreams - FREE prequel

Moonlight Mate (#1)

Wolf Untamed (#2) - coming 2022

Fae Chronicles

The Complete trilogy Boxset

Shadow of the Fae (#1)

Blood of the Fae (#2)

Revenge of the Fae (#3)

Thunderbird Academy

The Complete trilogy Boxset

Of Water and Moonlight (Thunderbird Academy, #1)

Of Destiny and Illusions (Thunderbird Academy, #2)

Of Storms and Triumphs (Thunderbird Academy, #3)

Hawthorne Chronicles

Guardian Witch (Hawthorne Chronicles, #1)

Witch's Fire (Hawthorne Chronicles, #2)

Witch's Heart (Hawthorne Chronicles, #3)

Tempest Witch (Hawthorne Chronicles, #4)

The Complete Season One Box Set

Predestined

The Titanium Trilogy

Pieces of Revenge (Titanium, #1)

Scarred by Vengeance (Titanium, #2)

Ruined in Retribution (Titanium, #3)

Complete Box Set

Falling Duology - YA contemporary romance

Falling by Design

Edge of Falling

Lightning Source UK Ltd.
Milton Keynes UK
UKHW010245170223
417160UK00018B/896/J